NK BROWN

Evernight Teen ®

www.evernightteen.com

THE UNITY EXPERIMENT

Copyright© 2025

NK Brown

ISBN: 978-0-3695-1113-3

Cover Artist: Jay Aheer

Editor: CA Clauson

NK BROWN

DEDICATION

For my family, both here and overseas. I love you, but yes, you are all characters in my story…

NK BROWN

THE UNITY EXPERIMENT

NK Brown

Copyright © 2025

Chapter One

Forty minutes until the lottery.

A marmoset stared down at me, frozen on a branch at the edge of the woods. Its sinewy fingers curled into the knotted bark, wide eyes eerily human. Drew shuffled closer, kicking at loose stones on the trail whilst muttering to himself, backpack dangling from his hand. I can't let him see it.

"You're late," I whispered, turning to face him. "Where have you been?"

"Anna, why do we have to do this now?" he said. "Let's just do it after … it."

My little brother struggles to call the vote by its real name, but that's okay. It was his way of processing, and he's only ten. I shouldered his school bag and tried to steer him away from the woods.

"What's that?" he asked.

"Nothing."

"Do you think it's—"

"No. It's just another illegal pet. Let's go."

Glancing back, the marmoset was still there, its intelligent eyes carefully watching our progress, processing *everything*. They always seemed to look directly at me, never at Drew, always unblinking, never appearing to even breathe. My fingers fumbled with his collar as I flipped it up to hide the throbbing pulse in his neck. Just in case.

We skirted around the forest as best we could, careful not to let even the shadows reach out and touch us. If we were the last ones left no one would be brave enough to come searching.

"Let's just go through the woods, it'll be—"

"No," I said.

"But then we'll skip the checkpoint, and they always smell me. It creeps me out." He stopped and tugged on my arm. "Please, Anna."

I sighed. "Not today, we can't risk it. Mother is going to want us all safely home and ready for the announcement." I squeezed him to me, his body as rigid as mine. "We have enough time. There's no reason for them to stop us. Okay?" We didn't have time—it was going to be tight.

He ducked out of my arm but remained glued to my heels.

A gust of wind rounded the corner and doused us in the stench of sweat and dank fur. Drew shivered next to me, and I took his hand. The fear in his wide eyes was plain to see, the anxiety gripping his skinny body. The usual bubbling of hatred re-awoke deep within me. If I could ease his pain in any way I would, but there was no escaping the curfew before the experiment and there was no escaping the vote. It was mandatory. Trapping a child in their home, the only place that they called safe, so they could be plucked out with ease if needed, was evil.

The forest penned us in on the right and on the left thick iron railings grew up into the sky. Six feet, eight feet, ten feet, the sharp arrow heads on top spearing the low clouds. Two burly men dressed entirely in black leather blocked the path. Both had long, wild brown hair and the unmistakable almond shape to their light brown eyes. Chunky annihilators were suspended from their belts, which were utterly pointless. Demi-beings didn't need fancy human weapons, even if the supernatural blood was weak. The taller man lifted his head, nostrils flaring as the edges of dark lips quirked. The other man's mouth hung open, tongue brushing against his teeth with a repetitive sucking noise.

I stepped forward allowing Drew to follow in my shadow. Holding out my hand palm up, the inky numbers of my human branding stood out clearly against the pale skin. The smaller guard pretended to squint with head cocked to the side, tongue still smacking in his open mouth.

Behind me, Drew whimpered.

With lightning speed, the guard snatched my hand and pressed it to his flared nostrils. He inhaled deeply, the delicate skin of my wrist exposed to his sharp white teeth. His eyes burned as they stared into mine and his long, wet tongue protruded slowly. The rough nodules dragged across my clammy palm as I fought to keep the look of disgust off my face. His tongue was ripped off me as the other guard's large fist savagely connected with the side of his head and they both stepped back, panting hard.

I remained frozen in place, heart pounding and stomach churning. Drew must see only my compliance. If I behaved, they would leave him alone. I lowered my arm and held it rigidly by my side. The skin burned where he had touched it, the overwhelming urge to rip my flesh off throbbed within me.

"Human girl G10 A650," the taller guard said. "You have missed the curfew."

"What? No, I haven't, there is still—"

My knees buckled as his hand slammed into my shoulder, crushing me onto the gravel. The marmoset was back in the tree again. A smile had crept onto its face, a curved slash on marble features.

There would be no help.

A radio crackled to life, its distorted buzz muffled by the tall man's leather jacket. He cocked his head, almond eyes never leaving mine as I stared up at him. A shadow crossed his face and dragged one corner of his mouth into a sneer.

"It's your lucky day, human," he whispered. He lowered his face until he was inches from mine. Stale breath coated my face, the stench of teeth that had not been brushed in days forced into my nostrils. "You're free to go after all."

I scuttled backward away from his hand, the rough skin of his fingers seared into bruises on my shoulder. Grabbing Drew, we sprinted through the checkpoint, not daring to turn around again. Nobody missed curfew and was allowed to pass.

Something was wrong.

Thirty minutes until the lottery.

We burst into the house and rushed straight into the living room. I sat on the floor, back pressed to the sofa and Drew huddled up next to me. The smell of salted bacon wafted from the kitchen carried by the weak rotations of the drooping ceiling fan. It was closely followed by the warming, seductive aroma of roasted chestnuts. There would be no changes this year. Mother was still having the family stick to the plan.

I stroked Drew's arm as we sat in silence, our

chests heaving and minds in overdrive. The radio was letting out a stream of infuriating chatter on the old brick fireplace. Every five minutes there would be a time call before delving into highlights from the previous experiment, all fabricated of course. If they had actually made any progress between the beings, then we would all be living in the blissful harmony that the governments wanted, co-existing without killing each other. Specifically, without us humans being killed anyway.

There has been an increasing amount of unrest after several suspicious disappearances, mainly around the fence in the east of the country. The Human Government has been under an enormous amount of pressure to agree to the terms of a new unity peace deal but...

I pushed myself up from the floor and grabbed the ornamental red pillow that my mother insisted remain safe on the worn sofa to make the room look more 'sophisticated'. The only way to improve this dismal room would be to burn everything in it. At least the smell of charred fabric would make an interesting change to the stale, musty odor that was permanently present.

New challenges have been introduced this year, designed to foster inter-species team building. The experiment must be a success! Our experts have predicted that we are barely holding the other beings at bay and there will soon be an all-out species war...

I placed the pillow over the radio and the angry buzzing mellowed into a soothing drone.

Twenty minutes until the lottery.

The front door slammed shut, briefly filling the house with the fresh spring air from outside. That would be my stepfather home. Our relationship had always been a functional one. One where we both pretty much leave each other alone and it works. This is the only day of the year when I feel any emotions toward him—gratitude mainly—as he nominates himself as a sacrifice for the whole family if we are chosen. That is what the chestnuts are for. If it is going to be his last meal with us, then my mother makes sure it is his favorite.

My younger sister stomped down the winding stairs. How she managed to make even her walk sound moody I have no idea. I could almost hear the flakes of paint being forced to let go of the ancient staircase, swirling with the dust in the lower hallway as her feet pounded the treads.

"All right, Drew," I said, "it's time. We should go wait in the kitchen ready for the vote."

The fear bounded back into his eyes. I took his hand and led him through the house, following the scent of the cooking food that was making my stomach churn.

The small, notched table took up most of the space in the tiny room. Five plain chairs were crammed around it, plates and glasses laid out in anticipation of the meal. The bacon sizzled in the center of the table, grease shining in the dull overhanging light that blanketed the room like a shroud. The chestnuts were piled high, steam waywardly floating into the air, dispersing the sweet scent through the tiny house.

Becky sat next to Mother, arms folded across her figure-hugging t-shirt. 'I love vampires' was stamped across it above a caricature of Dracula, complete with a crimson heart filling his otherwise barren chest. She liked to think that she was being open-minded, of championing the union between the beings, but she was just a silly girl. She had never met a vampire and would probably run away screaming or end up becoming its next meal if she did.

Well, none of us had, which was another reason why the lottery was a needless waste of life. No integration to be seen.

Ten minutes before the lottery.

A melodic chiming knifed through the silence and identical slender cylinders appeared, spaced out along the walls of the kitchen. I went robotically to mine, the orange colored one by the window. I glanced outside and saw the neighbor standing in front of a blue cylinder in his small kitchen. There was a look of indecision on his face. He'd had two years to think of a name, why was he so unsure now? His wife was a nasty piece of work, face like a shrew and temperament just as malicious. I would vote for her in a heartbeat if I could. He tugged on the dirty lace curtain that covered his window severing my view.

I turned my attention back to the cylinder. A white, rectangular strip of paper had appeared and a feathered quill with a razor-sharp nib. The feathers were each a different color to represent each of the beings and we were told everyone had to go through the same process, werewolves and mermaids alike. But in reality, who knew? Like any sham democracy, free thinkers and rebels were promptly executed. Or sometimes they found themselves publicly winning the lottery. What a convenient coincidence for the governments.

Every time the lottery was called, we voted the same. We had discussed it openly as a family and to try and remove some of the hurt and anxiety, especially for Drew, my stepfather told us to vote for him. He was the eldest, the strongest and would have the best, albeit still hopeless, chance of surviving.

It was easier for me, not being his biological child, but still, through the progression of the years and writing a death sentence on a scrap of paper—hoping it would never come true—was probably irrevocably taking its toll somewhere on my soul. I would probably end up materializing as a poltergeist, destined never to enjoy any part of the eternal hell that would be coming to me.

My mother, if she were turned into a ghost, would probably be an alms spirit. She did try her best to keep us afloat after the death of my real father and then to bring this blended family together. The only exception was a rather frantic six months after my father's death where I was left to pretty much fend for myself whilst she gallivanted off around the county looking for another partner. Obviously, I love her dearly, but she is a woman who is unable to be by herself. She needs a stronger presence around her, be it man, woman, or other entity.

And I was not enough.

Grasping the quill, I scratched my stepfather's name on the blank paper. It came out in blood-red ink, glowed briefly and then was sucked up the cylinder with another melodic chime. My tongue scratched around in my mouth—it was bone dry. Guilt compressed me, like a boulder on my chest, restricting me from taking proper breaths. I was doing what I was told, what we had all decided to do, but I still felt spineless.

My body slumped as I dragged myself back to the silent table. The five of us squeezed around it, cold shoulders touching, making the tiny kitchen feel like a shoebox. The walls slunk closer with every strained breath. Not here, not now. I had to breathe through the rising panic.

My heart raced as the claustrophobia tried to fight its way out.

Five minutes before the lottery.

Drew gripped my hand in his, he was ice cold to my red-hot sweating palm. His body shook as the panic overwhelmed his fragile being. I squeezed back, trying to calm him the only way I knew how, by being there for him. Becky limply took my other hand. The minimum amount of contact possible between her cinnamon scented moisturizer and ebony fingernails with my own hand was fine by me.

"Let us offer thanks as a family," my mother began quietly. Her voice was strong, her words clear, unflappable, as always. "For those who have valiantly tried and failed in the many years past and for those that are destined to fight and die for us tomorrow, so that we may all live in unity. All entities together in a peaceful world. Until death do us part."

"Until death do us part," we chanted after her.

Thirty seconds until the lottery.

The ancient cuckoo clock on the wall chimed 6:00. The flaking yellow door swung open and a small peasant with an axe squeaked out on rusted hinges. The blade raised in the air and then jerked down with a thud into a notched piece of gnarled firewood. He labored away, swinging the axe in an irritatingly regular rhythm. The sixth axe stroke was replaced by a booming thump on the front door.

My blood ran cold.

NK BROWN

Chapter Two

None of us moved.

The clock groaned and squeaked as the peasant was dragged back inside the mechanism, the small door slamming shut behind. Drew's hand was still clamped onto mine, a tingling starting in my fingers as the circulation was severed. My other hand was becoming damp and oily in Becky's manicured one. I would never get the scent out now, but she hadn't let go.

Another boom filled the room. This time it was not to be ignored. My stepfather kissed my mother's hand and raised himself slowly out of his chair. Another surge of respect for him washed over me. He walked confidently and without any hesitation. Surely, he knew what fate awaited him on the other side of the closed door?

A metallic grating fired into the house as the bolt was drawn back and the door opened. A huge, shiny black camera hovered in the doorway like the bulbous eye of a black widow spider, complete with a small red light blinking in the top corner. Next to it was a squirrel of a man. He had a serious, somber face and his black eyes darted around the room, analyzing everything. A pristine lab coat fell past his knees. His small hands nervously clutched a clipboard, the paper of which he kept smoothing obsessively.

"This is Dr MacAsher, announcing the volunteer from Grafton county, subsection 10."

His nasal voice was official, monotone and lacking any empathy. He collected himself, still repetitively smoothing the paper in his delicate hands and affected what he probably considered a more sympathetic tone, speaking slower and quieter. This time he addressed my stepfather in the doorway, eyes unable to focus on one target for any length of time.

"The government has high hopes this year for the success of the human race and the forging of peace between all the beings. Of course, without our volunteer subjects such a feat could never be possible."

The scientist paused, black eyes quickly checking the piece of paper in front of him, making sure he'd delivered the correct line. A flash of sympathy toward him dragged my gaze to the table.

"Ahem," he cleared his throat, the sound small and pathetic, "the nominee from the Smith family is…"

We were all still glued to our chairs, hands fastened in solidarity or in a desperate attempt at comfort, to ease the crippling guilt that smothered us. My sympathy for the scientist evaporated. The stoic figure of my stepfather stood patiently, hand on the doorknob, as if ready to slam it in the squirrel's face.

I wish he would.

The scientist stroked the paper one last time with a trembling finger. Yellowed teeth emerged from behind thin, dark lips as he bit down on flesh.

"Mable."

My stomach churned violently. Acidic bile carved its way up my throat. I stared at my mother. How could that be? She hadn't moved. Her face was expressionless, eyes locked with my stepfather who remained standing motionless by the door. I couldn't lose her as well.

"Oh, my." The scientist let out a small whimper. "Sorry for the confusion, folks." He reached into his breast pocket and pulled out a pair of thick rimmed glasses. He slid them on, black eyes suddenly magnified as he squinted back at the paper. "Mable *Anna* Smith. Seems you have the same first name."

I didn't process. I couldn't process. There was a

ringing in my ears, a stabbing pain in my chest. Becky dropped my hand and it slid limply onto the table, my nails sinking deep into the familiar notches. The room shrank again. The ceiling fan pressed down from above, the smell of roasted chestnuts now suffocating.

From far away the voice resumed its methodical commentary to the camera. "Volunteer subject human girl G10, goes by her middle name of Anna. Five feet two, one hundred and twenty pounds, seventeen years of age. No known associations with any other beings, no ties to any governments. Will be randomly assigned to a team once processed."

The red light in the camera died. The scientist ducked his head and scuttled backward out of view. The same two guards from the checkpoint loomed in the doorway.

They used to televise the whole experiment, from revelation to death. But too many humans decided not to play along. Too many times the annihilators had been used and rather than have the desired effect of acting like a deterrent, they did the opposite. A quick, easy end rather than the prolonged terror that was coming. A large part of me did not blame them either. But the government decided instead to record live only for the experiment scientists and broadcast a carefully edited montage to the rest of the population. Somehow all the 'volunteers' seemed to make it to the start after that.

The taller guard stood back with hands hooked into his belt and a satisfied smirk stretched across his face. The other slowly licked his lips as saliva drooled from his mouth. He sucked it back in and grinned at me.

My leg bounced against the table leg, and I forced my clammy hand down onto my thigh to stop the movement. Demi-beings fed off fear.

I wasn't seen as a threat. A small, young woman,

frozen in terror, still clutching her little brother's hand. The grinning guard came forward. The heavy tread of his metal-toed boots echoed through the room, the tired linoleum floor offering no resistance to his path. A rough, haired hand grabbed my upper arm. The coarseness burned my skin through my long-sleeved sweater. Drew's hand was forced from mine, releasing a torrent of tears which slid down his face as he silently choked back sobs.

My feet were moving. The fresh spring air was getting closer as I left the dank kitchen behind. Not a word was uttered. No goodbye, no futile words of encouragement or of hope. I would never return to this house, to the county, to the human section. Everyone knew it.

A small boxcar with blackened windows waited at the entrance to the tunnels just outside our house. I tried to avoid traveling by underground as much as possible. It was like traveling in a coffin with a hundred feet of dirt and stones precariously balanced on top of you, just asking to fail and bury you alive. The small light inside the boxcar made things worse. Then there was no pretending just how tight a space you were forced into.

The taller guard opened the door and pointed inside with a nod of his head. An air of disappointment surrounded him. One hand still rested hopefully on the weapon by his side, his brown eyes scrutinizing my every breath looking for the smallest act of defiance.

The guard gripping my arm hovered over me. Fresh saliva trickled out of his open mouth and dripped onto my shoulder. I wrenched out of his grasp and stepped inside the boxcar slamming the door shut behind me.

I pressed myself as deeply into the corner as I could, putting my hands flat on the wall and sliding down to the floor. The rumbling and creaking vibrated through my bones as the boxcar lowered through the thick concrete roof. The wind rushed past my face and my stomach soared into my mouth as I plunged into the depths of the underground. I kept my hands firmly planted on the trembling walls and eyes tightly shut.

The reason I was petrified of small spaces was solely down to one of my father's many experiments. He had shut me in a wooden box one day. Literally nailed it shut. Every hammer blow became duller and duller as the light faded and the darkness torqued around me. The air had stagnated, frozen in horror like I was at the forced captivity.

He never told me the purpose it was supposed to serve. Only that it had failed. I had failed. Then it was my mother who cleaned the blood from my torn fingers, buffed nails that had been scratched to jagged points and fed me honeyed water for the trench-like furrows carved into my throat by my unanswered screams. It was one of the few days when she showed any maternal instinct toward me, and I had gravitated toward her instead of my father.

My lasting impression of my father and my favorite way to describe him to people is 'odd'. There are other adjectives I could use like experimental, eccentric, open, fair. But *odd* will always be my fallback description. I could describe my parents' marriage in the same way. It was never happy, but neither did it seem like a match of pure convenience. My mother, I was sure, secretly hated him, but over time I began to think maybe the emotion was fear instead. After all, she was there the day he nailed me into that box and hadn't done anything to stop it.

By contrast, she is a lot brighter now and I, by equal measure, am a lot duller. Every day I wished I could step back in time and hit pause. Watch the movie of our lives jerk to a stop, when there were just the three of us. Then throw away the remote and exist in that eternal freeze-frame.

The radio crackled to life. I listened to the uninvited prattle, trying to distract myself from my swirling thoughts.

Welcome, human research subject G10. You will shortly be transported to the start of the experiment where you will join your teammates…

The vibrations slowed and my stomach settled as I reached the deepest part. Now began the labyrinth of twists and turns. A roller coaster in the pitch black, squeezing through tightly packed tunnels like a rat in a maze.

What had happened? Had there been a mistake? I should have received no votes. My stepfather, per the agreement, would vote for my mother, as you couldn't elect yourself. When had the plan changed? She had cooked the chestnuts after all, the signal we used as a family for every lottery.

How many years had someone been voting for me?

The bile rose again in my throat. I swallowed it down, relishing the burn. At least it was a distraction to the tornado of thoughts rocketing around in my head.

You will need to work together to overcome a series of challenges designed to test the ability of our species to work together, even in the most difficult of…

My father had done this exact same journey ten years ago. Math had never been my strong suit, but even I knew the odds of both of us being selected were infinitesimal. I had always harbored a sense of injustice at his being taken from me. Directed it toward the government, toward my teachers and then toward my mother.

There was a screech of brakes and my fingernails scrabbled for purchase on the walls, splinters of wood digging deeply into my skin. Squeezing pressure filled my ears, my eye sockets, my head. I gritted my teeth and pushed back against the unrelenting walls harder. The breath was sucked out of me as the boxcar catapulted back up toward the earth.

We are confident that this year will be a success. The surviving team providing the missing link our scientists need to...

The outer motion of the boxcar jerked to a stop, but my head still spun. I threw my hands over my face as a scorching ray of sunlight lasered directly into my retinas, the streaks tattooed onto my eyelids. Slowly I blinked my eyes open, squinting into the bright square of light coming from the open door. Pushing up from the walls, I straightened my stiff legs and wobbled out onto the platform.

This was not a usual platform junction as there were no signposts, and it was completely deserted. The door of the boxcar slammed shut behind me and the metallic screeching resumed as it was lowered back down into the tunnels. I let out my breath and spread my hands wide, stretching into the air. I felt so much lighter and more stable, now I was free again. Back above ground where humans belonged.

The junction was in the middle of a deserted field of poppies. The small flowers waved slowly in the light spring breeze, a delicious floral scent washing over me. Ironically the poppy was previously seen as the symbol of unity between the beings, but now it served as a trigger. A reminder of the suspicions and war and deaths that occurred before the separation.

The comforting sounds of silence crept around, stilling the whirring of my mind and relaxing my tense muscles. I plucked one of the flowers from the dry ground, inhaling its perfume. The scent changed as the breeze increased in intensity, now gusting and pushing around me. The harsh, toxic odor of kerosine filled my nostrils, burning out the calming floral notes. Tucking the poppy into my jeans pocket, I covered my ears as the roar of an engine replaced the tranquility. A huge cargo plane descended onto the field, annihilating the innocent flowers in its path.

The instant it stopped, a burly woman jumped out of the front door and marched toward me. She was carrying a small crimson burlap sack, a chunky annihilator and a look of disgust. Her thin mouth was pursed together, giving it the appearance of a duck bill. She placed a skin-colored strip of fabric over the bridge of her nose as she neared me.

"Human subject G10?" Her voice was nasal and shrill.

I nodded at her. She opened the bag and using only her fingertips threw a pair of red gloves at me. I put them on, and my hands snapped together with a sharp click. I wriggled my fingers inside the coarse fabric and tried to pull my hands apart, but they were bound tight.

"You are the last collection. Next stop, the start."

"How wonderfully informative," I muttered.

A tutting sound escaped the duck bill and she reached into the bag again, lurid green fingernails holding the edges of a matching red hood. She took a deep breath and then stepped close to me, flinging the hood over my head. The coarse fabric instantly melted into my face, smothering me. My heart raced as I tried to breathe in, just sucking airless fabric into my mouth instead of oxygen. But quick as it came, the fabric melted away from my nose and mouth. Gasping in the kerosine-tainted air gratefully, I just stood there, unable to see anything except for a sheet of crimson.

"Follow me, volunteer." When I didn't move, the nasal voice added sarcastically, "Just walk straight."

I stumbled blindly forward, trying to pick my feet up high to avoid the remaining flowers. My foot caught on a raised ledge, and I hit the ground hard, unable to break my fall, bound hands crushed uselessly under my body. A trickle of blood seeped from my nose and spilled into my mouth. The last thing I wanted was to be bleeding when thrown to the mercy of my teammates. That was the fastest way to end up dead.

The scent of fuel was stronger now and mixed with the smell of sweat and fear. I pushed up as best as I could and carefully crept up the ramp to the plane, a hollow echo following. The stale, warm air pressed in around me as I entered what was presumably the hold and fumbled my way along a wall, searching for the familiar comfort of a corner.

The deafening roar of the engines receded as we took to the sky, and I was left acutely aware of the others.

NK BROWN

Chapter Three

A muffled sound of tears came from my left, the choking sound filtered through a coarse barrier. To my right came a moan, broken only by sniffles and a wet cough. I pressed deeper into the cold metal wall, wishing I was able to cover my ears and stop their emotions penetrating deep into my soul.

"No mermaids this year, such a shame." A drooling voice began, ignoring the sobbing echoing across the large space. "I was hoping to make a bit of a splash, wet my whistle, as they say."

He gave a disgusting chuckle, and I pulled my knees in closer, hugging my bound hands around them.

"I'm surprised they were given the pass." This speaker was a woman. She had a motherly voice, soothing and calming. I bet she was a schoolteacher, a classroom full of eager, hopeful faces cheering her on, oblivious to the futility of her task. They were probably making a collage of messy drawings, stick figures hugging zombies and taking tea with angels. Giving false hope to the young who didn't know any better.

She continued, "The last one did nothing except toss his long, shiny hair in the sun and pout into the camera. Should have been annihilated right from the beginning if you ask me."

Maybe not a schoolteacher after all. She was right, though. Every year one of the beings was awarded the *honor* of the title 'Vessel of Unity'. Even if their team all perished and there were no overall winners, which happened frequently, they would be plucked out of the zones before they could be killed and given a free pass. Usually, the only way to escape and return home would be to win. But this strategy was devised as an extra incentive to stop the beings of the same team from killing each other immediately once the human was killed. Then the Vessel of Unity—and yes, it is a ridiculously stupid name, invented by an elf, of course—meant that the entire species was then exempt from the next lottery.

Humans had never yet won.

A third voice joined in the conversation, loud and authoritative. "There wasn't much of a gap between these two lotteries, barely two years. They must not have gleaned any meaningful data from the last experiment. I heard they were increasing the number of teams this year to try and force a winner through sheer numbers."

My arms flew into the air as the plane dropped suddenly, unable to reach out and stop the momentum. Wedged into the corner I was more stable than some of the others and heard the thuds of bodies rolling around on the metal floor. The engine roared back to life again, the vibrations reverberating through my whole body, chattering the teeth in my skull.

The plane leveled out, returning the stilted conversations with it.

The loud voice resumed, "I was first in, being from county A and we've made nine stops since then. So twice as many as last time."

"Double the blood on their hands this year," the schoolteacher said, and I silently agreed with her.

"Who cares about the fucked-up logic of the Human Government," the first voice spoke again. "It's good they are taking more of us. They came trolling around the prisons for volunteers and had more sign ups than expected. I was lucky, my warder vouched for me. The official line was that I had more self-control than the others and would hover within the guidelines of the experiment. But really, the guy hates the idea of mixing with the others as much as me. For every one of them that

I kill, he's going to send a reward to my fiancé. That's the kind of incentive that works."

"That is not the point of the experiment." This voice was quiet but determined.

"Of course it's the point. Kill or be killed. Jesus, you're not entering to actually make a difference, are you?" He gave another scornful chuckle.

Interested, I turned my attention toward the quiet voice. I pictured a small, young woman, slight, but strong, maybe an activist. The kind that protested peacefully, not needing to shout or paint signs in faux blood to get attention. But one that still commanded attention. That made you avert your eyes in shame, knowing that they were a much better person than you are.

"My partner and I are both entering. The only way for us to be together is for the unity to be a success."

"Well, you are both going to end up dead," the schoolteacher said, ending the conversation.

I really wanted to ask her more. I had never heard of any human meeting with another being since the separation. Especially one that had not only survived to tell the tale but also fell in love at the same time. But the plane lapsed into silence again, my chance gone.

My father often told me stories about the other beings. Of the charm of the mermaids, the poetry of the centaurs, the unheard messages of the spirits. He always championed the union, publicly loathed the segregation and loudly advocated for the freedom to fall in love with whomever the soul chose.

Mother always shut him down, told him not to plant weeds in my head or they would overgrow. But it was too late, the roots having already sprouted.

I didn't want to be here, travelling to certain death, but I was curious to meet with the others. Learn their stories, watch them move, interact, think. Maybe my final thoughts would be how wrong the Human Government was—and then how right I was never to believe the propaganda—until they silenced me for it.

We were never shown how my father died nor given proof of his death and the conspiracy theorist in me blamed it on him being forcibly silenced. Despite his odd experiments, he was a good man, and brave. He would never have gone against the truth and that would have made him many enemies. I would follow in his footsteps as far as I could, maybe overtake them, maybe step aside to form my own, but here was my chance to find out what really happened. What games did the government play?

Eventually the persistent but rhythmic sounds of the sobbing to my left started to take effect. My eyelids grew heavy, and my breathing deepened. I tuned out all the other noises and began to drift off. The final image in my head was the small kitchen, the bacon still sizzling on the table. It was my father's favorite food. My mother thought it was mine as well, but I only requested it because the smell reminded me of him. A pang of loneliness pulsed in my heart, threatening to burst through the tacked seam once again.

This must be how he felt when it was his turn.

Chapter Four

Forcing my legs to move, I creaked into a standing position, still firmly wedged in the corner. The announcement had come four times already and this time the nasal voice said 'Red' which I took to be myself. Another heavier set of footsteps moved across the floor of the plane and stopped next to me. The rich scent of fresh leather and stale cigarettes blended into a mixture which made me wish my nostrils were still crusted shut with blood.

My bound hands were forced up and attached to something solid in front of me with a loud zipping sound which dragged me forward and out of the safety of the corner. I stumbled but was prevented from falling by the object in front. A human man I was certain. A teammate? An enemy? A decoy? It was time to stop feeling sorry for myself and focus.

A heavy weight attached to my back, skewing my center of gravity. The crimson mask staining my eyelids peeled off slowly, pulling and tugging on the cold skin underneath. I had a brief glimpse of sharp brown eyes and an aquiline nose before the door to the plane was flung open and we were both sucked outside.

My lungs burned and my throat closed as the wind rushed by me. My heart hammered in my chest and my legs thrashed wildly, unable to find any purchase. Everything blurred as tears obscured my vision. Only the crimson gloves directly in front of my face were recognizable, the only constant that I could cling to in the howling and cackling of the wind that dragged me down.

My hands were thrust toward my face, and I tried to jerk my head back, but the pressure of the wind was like a brace, crushing my head down onto my shoulders.

My hands tugged clumsily on the skin beneath my eyes, but I wasn't ordering them to move. As the tears were absorbed by the rough fabric, the deep brown eyes appeared again in front of me. His mouth moved frantically, pearly white teeth clashing together. No noise reached my ears through the roaring of the wind. I tried to focus on the movement of his mouth, the shapes forming behind lips that curled down naturally at the edges.

Pull.

Pull what? My hands were forced up and to my left and a red ribbon appeared in the corner of my vision. It was braided in a long, strong coil and flapped violently. I wrenched my hands toward it, dragging the man's hands with me and wrapped my fingers around it. The cherry-colored fabric cut through the gloves and into the skin of my hands. I pulled, ignoring the burn of my flesh. The man wrapped his strong legs around my waist which is when I realized he did not have a parachute. He was only attached by the gloves.

Velvety red fabric punched out of the small pack as the gloves binding us were ripped apart by the momentum. He dug his fingers deep into the flesh of my arms and I grabbed the front of his shirt. The last of my breath was forced from my lungs as we slammed to a halt, suspended over a thick green canopy of trees.

The deafening rush of air ceased as a beautiful silence enveloped us. Blood still pounded around my battered body and sweat ran from my slippery palms inside the thick gloves dripping down my arms before soaking into my sweater, but suddenly the world was beautiful again.

I let out a hysterical burst of laughter, the sound hoarse and foreign from my raw throat. The man's legs were still locked around me, like a boa constrictor around a fawn. He didn't smile. His lips were pursed together, a muscle pulsing in his cheek, tension causing the tendons of his neck to pop out from the collar of his pristinely pressed shirt. How did he still look perfect? I could guarantee that my hair was spilling out everywhere, blood still smeared on my face, creases permanently embedded into my clothes.

"What took you so long to pull the cord?" he snapped, the odor of cigarettes swirling into my mouth.

The plush canopy below us drifted closer, bringing with it a warm humidity. The faint sound of unrecognizable animals cackled in the distance. I didn't answer. I didn't want to admit that the panic had completely overtaken me, and I would be dead on the ground right now if it wasn't for him. Any gratitude I may have felt evaporated instantly as his eyes bored into mine.

He was probably ten years older than me, somewhere in his late twenties, and it was plain he was government. Lower levels, of course, otherwise he wouldn't have been in the lottery. Despite the warm air I shivered as a chill spread through me.

"Do you speak?" he said. "You must do as you managed to scream all the way down."

I glared at him. My fingers dug deeper into the fabric of his shirt to stop my hands from pushing him off me. At this height, he may not die if I let him go. Probably not worth it.

He let out a frustrated breath. "Well, we are paired together, for better or worse. So, you should get your act together."

"What are you talking about?" I managed to croak out.

"Two humans in a team this year. Increases the odds of at least one surviving."

We crashed through the leafy canopy. Huge

droplets of rain showered down as the green fronds were forced aside. A sharp pain scored down my leg as a wayward branch tried to impale me. I landed heavily with a wet thump, initially on my feet, before the weight of the man still clinging on to me forced me backward.

He landed on top of me compressing my chest, and I struggled to suck in a breath. I could taste the fresh cotton on his shirt collar as it was pressed over my face laced with the poisonous stench of cigarettes. I wriggled and tried to free my arms to push him off me, but he was too heavy. Panic welled in my chest.

I sank my teeth deep into the soft fabric of his shoulder. It wasn't hard enough to taste blood or even to penetrate the meaty layers of muscle, but he shrieked and the pressure on my chest lightened.

I drew in a deep, thankful breath allowing the thick, damp smells of the jungle to flood my senses. Noises were everywhere and yet it was oddly silent around us. The place hummed, it throbbed, it felt alive.

High above in the green canopy, perched secretly on a gnarled branch, was the fireman red plumage of a scarlet macaw. Its black, beady eyes peered down at me, razor sharp talons digging into the soft tree bark. A brief flashback sparked, of the marmoset in the woods. The apathy in its expression was only a ruse, barely concealing centuries worth of cunning beneath.

"Jesus, what is wrong with you?"

Another sharp pain appeared in my side as his boot connected with my ribs. Groaning, I rolled over and forced myself to stand. The trees spun and danced around me, and I clutched at the nearest one. Digging my fingers into the textured bark, ignoring the small splinters embedding under my nails, I let out a long breath and waited for the spinning to stop.

A colony of fire ants marched down the tree,

steering a wide path around my hands. Their identical bodies, fat and round, all swayed in perfect unison to an imaginary beat. Why were they going the wrong way? Following the trail back up the tree, my eyes met the unnerving glare of the macaw again. The bird had not moved, even the feathers on its chest were still. I looked away, rubbing the raised hairs on my arms.

The man continued to glare at me, holding pathetically to his injured shoulder. A faint trace of dried blood stained his white shirt where I'd bitten him. I wiped my damp sleeve over my face and managed to shrug at him whilst biting back the manic laughter that was about to explode out of me. The look on his face was priceless.

"I'm Chris. Where are the others?" He looked around and then down at his watch impatiently. "We should get notice of the start any time now. We're not going to get very far just the two of us."

He gave me a condescending look as he slowly took in my disheveled form. I rolled my eyes in response.

Now the jungle had stopped spinning I could take in the surroundings. We were in a wide clearing. The floor was littered with fallen leaves and sticks, and the air seemed to shimmer as the warm rain evaporated into a thick, swirling mist. Beneath the fresh smell of rain was a sickly, rotting odor that lingered in my nostrils and coated the inside of my mouth. There was a very soft, swishing noise in the distance. It sounded like a ball gown, the layers of fabric rustling together as the dancer glided over the floor.

"I don't think we are alone," I eventually answered him, the eyes of the macaw still boring into me from above.

"Well, I can't see anyone else. What we really need is for the spirit to materialize. That is how we are going to be given the information we need."

I blinked at him. "What do you mean?"

He gave a dramatic sigh, his neatly styled brown hair hardly moving as he shook his head. "Didn't you listen to the briefing?"

I shrugged. I had no idea what he was talking about.

"What have they done to me?" he murmured, briefly closing his eyes.

I glared at him, anger beginning to bubble up inside. We stood in silence for a while before he took a deep breath and tried again at making conversation.

"So, what are you good at?"

I shrugged again. His superior attitude and air of authority was going to make this difficult. I felt a childish impulse to see how far I could push him.

His eyes narrowed and he folded his arms across his chest. "Can you shoot a weapon?"

"Probably." I had never tried.

"Can you run fast, hide well, climb trees?"

"The only thing I have ever climbed are the stairs."

I bit back a grin as he closed the gap between us. He was easily a foot taller than me and whilst not muscular, he still managed to be imposing as he loomed over.

"This is not a joke. Do you want to die out here?"

I met his gaze and with some difficulty managed to not roll my eyes at him.

"Good," he said.

I remembered the backpack that was attached to me before the jump and reached back, tearing it from my sweater. Inside there were two loaded annihilators, I grabbed one, the metal now warm and slippery in the humidity.

"Here," I said, as I threw it at him.

It bounced off his folded arms and he stared at me as he bent to pick it up from the floor. He tucked it carefully into the waistband of his black leather trousers. I put the other one in my jeans and reached back into the pack. Inside were two identical canteens, both brick red, and an assortment of dried food.

He pressed closer again, until he was standing uncomfortably near, body casting a shadow over mine. Fresh drops of sweat ran down his smooth face and dripped onto my gloved hands as he peered into the pack.

"We'll need to ration this. I'll take it."

The supplies were wrenched out of my hands, and he pressed the red pack against his back, a soft metallic click echoing through the clearing as it attached.

The swishing sound in the background was becoming louder, coming closer. On the tree beside me, the line of fire ants was continuing their march. They seemed to have picked up the pace, hurrying down the bark and off into the jungle. In the opposite direction to the approaching noise.

"Maybe we should wait somewhere else?"

The sweat trickled down my back, but despite the heat, it was cold. My heart beat faster, matching the increased pace of the ants' tiny footfalls. I watched them leave, jealousy flaring.

"No," he answered.

The rustling, swishing sound crept even closer. Now even he couldn't pretend not to hear its approach. He threw his head from side to side, trying to locate the direction. His eyes were wide, nostrils flared as he scanned the shadows outside of the clearing. Even the ants had broken rank and were now fleeing in panic. The temperature had risen significantly, the stench of rotting flesh overpowering. I gagged quietly, afraid to make a noise.

Then silence fell.

The only sound was the hammering of my heart, the pounding of blood in my veins. I stopped breathing and the burn crept into my chest.

Then I flew backward, smashed into the floor, the green of the trees smothered by a hairy black thorax. Red claws speared through my limbs, skewering me to the damp ground.

I had a brief glimpse of dozens of unblinking glazed eyes before two ivory fangs plunged into my shoulder.

Chapter Five

My raw throat burned as I screamed, arms flailing, trying to push it off me. The claws pierced through my upper arms and legs, blood bubbling out of the wounds. The fangs plunged and tore at the flesh of my shoulder, a fierce burning spreading down my right arm. Blood laced drool congealed and slapped down onto my face in chunks. I was going to die. Its black eyes focused on me, and through the searing pain and blinding panic I knew that I wasn't ready. I hadn't lived.

The poison oozed through my veins, the burning replaced by an intense itching. I wanted to rip the skin off my right side, rid my body of the writhing fire ants burrowing deep within me. My left hand twitched and grasped something slippery and hard. My fingers weakly closed around it, strength starting to leave my body. Barely able to move, I pointed the square nozzle blindly at the giant creature pulsating over me and pressed the trigger.

The shock waves rippled through the damp jungle, leaves and branches flung through the sky. The resounding boom left me with a piercing ringing in my ears, my eyelids clamped shut to try and stop the noise. The pain was all consuming. Singed flesh splattered onto me, hair and bone raining down all around.

Before I could drag in vital breath, I was flying. Forcibly held upright and pressed back into the tree. An ice-cold hand wrapped around my neck and another sharp stabbing assaulted my shoulder. My eyes flew open as a sucking, squelching noise filled my ringing ears, like boots stuck in the mud.

The black eyes of the macaw narrowed dangerously at me, warning me not to move. The scarlet feathers had been replaced with short flame-red hair, framing a pale face and alabaster smooth skin smeared with blood. My blood. She paused, fangs tugging out of my shredded shoulder and slowly licked her lips. Her head snapped back, ready to feed again and I braced myself for the pain.

A gust of wind slashed across my face and her marble hand was forced from my throat. Unable to move or comprehend what had happened, I gulped in air and weakly gripped the rough bark of the tree behind me.

The shapeshifter stood angrily brushing dirt off her figure-hugging jumpsuit in the center of the clearing. Her black eyes smoldered, focused on something just behind me. "I wasn't going to kill her." Her voice was smooth, melodic and beautiful. "She'll be more useful now without the poison from that creature ripping her apart. It would have been an agonizing process. We never would have heard the end of it as one by one her extremities burned off." She paused and one corner of her mouth twitched upward as she met my gaze. "And I needed a good feed." Her tongue flicked out again and ran over her lower lip, soaking up a smear of crimson blood.

I looked down at my arm. The sleeve of my sweater was completely missing, my skin from shoulder to fingertips deathly pale, covered in coalescing black and blue bruises. Dark red blood congealed over four messy slashes, just below my collarbone. The rusty, iron-rich smell was overwhelming. A new heat grew inside me as I processed what had happened.

"Why didn't you shoot it?" I spun toward Chris.

He was standing off to the side, one hand gripping the unused annihilator that I had thrown at him only moments ago, pale face glistening with sweat.

"I only have five pulses," he said with a small

shrug, "you seemed to be ok."

I started to raise the barrel again. The ringing was back in my ears and anger was creeping up my body. A hot, strong hand gripped my arm, hairs rough against my skin. Glancing down to rip it off me, I paused, noticing the letters RED tattooed on the knuckles. I looked up again and the almond-shaped eyes of the being materialized from behind the tree. My whole body jerked as if I had been shocked, my brain suddenly firing only blank thoughts into my mind, blank except for those golden eyes.

"Not yet," he whispered.

I don't know why he calmed me or why I obeyed, but I did as he ordered. Shoving the annihilator back in my waistband, I shot Chris an irritated look.

The bark of the tree scratched my aching back as I slid down. My body having finally given up the fight, I rested on the slick ground, gloved hands slipping into a slimy mess of saliva, blood and sweat.

I looked around the clearing. This must be the rest of the red team. Another figure had joined and sat perched in the lowest branches of a drooping tree, long silver hair shimmering and glittering in the shadows. She was wearing a necklace of red leaves but was otherwise camouflaged with the strong greens and browns of the forest.

"We should be getting an announcement soon and the spirit should be communicating directly with me, as your leader." Chris spoke, his voice echoing in the now stillness of the space.

I think you should have shot him.

The voice appeared in my head. Red text on a black background, materializing as if typed on an old-fashioned typewriter. I looked around the clearing. No one had spoken aloud and none of the others seemed to have heard anything. The sixth and final member must have arrived.

Chris continued, oblivious to the narrowed eyes and pursed lips of those listening. "None of you would have been told any of this information of course," the corners of his mouth twitched down as he smiled, "but as a government official I have a lot of insider knowledge that is going to prove very useful."

The woman in the tree hopped down lightly, feet not making a sound as she landed and glided over to him. She placed a delicate hand on his arm and her face broke out into a radiant smile. "I feel blessed to have you lead this team, Chris." Her voice seemed entwined with the wind, it came from every direction at once and yet from nowhere. "We all agree, no?"

The blush rose in his face, and he swallowed. He was staring into her twinkling purple eyes and seemed to have forgotten about everyone else.

What an idiot. There is still time. Shoot him now.

I snorted and then clamped my gloved hand over my mouth as everyone turned to me. I pretended to cough, but Chris's brown eyes burned into mine.

He recovered himself. "So, let's see who we have on the red team." He looked around and began listing everyone, speaking as if they were pieces of fruit at a grocery store. "A vampire."

"Shapeshifter," I corrected.

He ignored me and continued. "Half-blood."

A low growl sounded from behind the tree.

"Werewolf," I corrected again.

"Pixie, of course," he gave the beautiful woman a coy smile. I rolled my eyes. He turned his gaze to me, one eyebrow raised, "And two..." he paused, his eyes raking over me, *"humans."*

Correction. One human. One asshole.

I snorted again, unable to disguise this one as an innocent cough.

"Where is the spirit?" He looked around.

"They're here," I answered him.

He narrowed his eyes and studied me again. Obviously, he didn't believe me because he continued scanning the clearing for whatever shape he had decided the spirit should take.

"Are you speaking in the heads of the others as well?" I whispered into the thick air, moisture condensing on my tongue as warm droplets as I spoke. "Because I don't hear them talking to themselves like idiots."

No. Just yours.

"Why?" I asked, feeling a rush of pleasure at being chosen.

Because your mind is the emptiest.

"Get out!" I hissed.

Chris strode over and stood with arms tightly folded, scowl on his face, looking down at me. The werewolf silently crept forward from behind the tree. Waves of tension pulsated around us. His low growl made the hair on the back of my neck stand up. But not from fear.

The pixie leapt delicately forward and raised a translucent hand. "You had better change back into your human form." It was a command, but so beautifully persuasive that I doubted anyone would ever resist. "You will need to control yourself throughout the experiment or you'll end up killing one of the humans. It is our task to protect them. You don't want to forget your promise, no?"

What she really meant to say is, if the werewolf kills one of you then her mission will be a failure. The magic folk are not known for their altruism, so don't be fooled.

I watched, fascinated, as the course auburn fur of the large creature beside me evaporated, replaced by golden brown skin and surprisingly normal clothing. The honey-colored almond eyes remained, aggressively boring into her purple ones.

Wiping my disgusting hands on a clean patch of damp moss beside me, I staggered to my feet. The strong hand of the werewolf reappeared again and held my upper arm, taking most of my weight with very little effort. He gripped too hard, lifting me as if I were a doll, but another shock of pleasure thrummed through me at his touch. He let go, but remained standing right next to me, breath hot on my neck.

"Where is the spirit?" Chris demanded.

I was starting to feel trapped again as he loomed over me from the front. The tree blocked my escape from behind and the werewolf hemmed me in on the right. My heart beat faster and, as if in harmony with my emotions, his low growl reverberated through the air again.

"Erm, in my head," I said.

"Your head?"

The scorn in his voice was infuriating. I wish I could have growled at him too.

The pixie spoke again, "I can sense its presence as well but don't know exactly what we are dealing with until it chooses to show itself. For now, the girl can keep it."

"I don't think I have a choice," I muttered.

Correct. Smarter than you look.

The macaw reappeared and sat in the tree above, head cocked, one beady eye fixed on me. An unnerving smear of red lined her beak. A spasm of pain shot through my shoulder, and I cried out, clutching at the wound.

"We'll find you some herbs and make a poultice when we start, yes?" the pixie said.

I groaned, "Haven't we already started?"

She smiled a blinding smile at me, perfect teeth snow white against the pastel pink of her lips. "Not yet, girl."

"Anna," I corrected.

"I know."

See. Total bitch.

I smiled wanly and turned to the werewolf. "What's your name?"

"Dylan." His voice was a whisper. Low and throaty like his growl but calming.

The pixie pointed upward toward the macaw and said, "Amura. We don't have names so you can call me Pixie if it makes you feel more comfortable, yes?"

I forced another smile which probably looked like a smirk. I don't know why I bothered—she could see straight through me anyway.

The spirit was speaking words again into my mind. The instructions for zone five had finally been sent. I repeated them out loud, fixing on a spot of bushy ferns in the distance to avoid the scrutinizing glares from around me.

Welcome to zone five and the start of the Unity Experiment. This will be the most challenging section of the experiment that you will face. Only one team may complete all five zones and return to their world. All members of the winning team must be alive or in their original forms at completion.

Red team, you have twelve hours to locate and retain the Vessel of Unity. Whichever team wields it when the time ends will be able to bestow it upon one of their team members, for use as they wish.

Thank you for your courage in volunteering to work together to bring unity between the entities and peace to our world.

NK BROWN

Now go and kill each other.
I didn't repeat the last part.

Chapter Six

The jungle hummed and pulsed around me, alive with colors and sounds. Pixie and Chris moved away as she whispered to him. Glad of the space, I sighed. Dylan was watching me suspiciously, not having moved from my shoulder. I turned away quickly as an awareness of his intense gaze brushed through me and a blush rose in my face.

"Hey, Chris," I called. "Can I have the water?"

He turned around and stared haughtily at me, raising one eyebrow.

"For fuck's sake," I muttered, "*please.*"

Dylan let out a soft growl of laughter next to me. I didn't look at him as my cheeks reddened more. Chris threw one of the cannisters toward me. My gloves slipped on the metal as I grabbed for it, and it smacked into my stomach instead. I let out a forced breath and glowered at him.

"Are you ready to kill people then?" Chris asked, a smirk creeping across his face.

"Of course I'm not going to kill anyone."

"You've only got four pulses left. You may need to ask your bodyguard there for advice."

My hand twitched by my side, waiting for permission to smack him. I knew I looked embarrassed, but maybe it would pass off for anger instead.

Pixie trilled a small laugh into the wind. "It's probably better that the two of you don't speak if you are going to antagonize one another, no? We have a long way to go yet."

God, did I hate her too. At least Dylan seemed to agree with me on that one. Whenever she spoke, his whole body tensed up beside me.

"Why is it so important that we need to get the vessel? Other than because we have been told to?" I asked. "We could just cruise through to zone four, all alive and somewhat happy."

"No, girl."

Every time Pixie didn't call me by my name, an invisible notch was removed from my resolve of peace.

She continued, "We need it. It not only bestows immunity to the species of the holder, which would be very useful to the humans who have never yet been excluded from the experiment, yes?" She didn't wait for a response. "But gives the holder a first-class ticket into the unity negotiations between the governments. That is, of course, the purpose of the experiment, no? Maybe you would be wise to discuss this further with your spirit friend, whilst the rest of us form a strategy."

"I agree with Anna. I want nothing to do with any of the governments," Dylan said, folding his arms across his chest.

Pixie looked at him, the smile not quite reaching her eyes which had darkened to indigo. "You don't need to worry about the reasons, wolf. Your only job, as has so rightfully been pointed out," she inclined her head toward Chris who didn't even try to hide the smug expression on his face, "is to guard the weak ones. Play to your strengths, yes?"

He bared his teeth, anger flashing in his eyes.

"There will be plenty of opportunities for you to release that tension. We will eliminate any of the others that we find as we go. You can take the lead on that, yes?"

"There is still no reason to kill anyone," I said.

The annihilator sat heavy, tucked into my jeans. I had never thought of myself as a pacifist before, but equally had never considered the meaning of actually taking a being's life.

"I don't expect you to be able to do it, girl," Pixie said. "As has been pointed out to you already, and you really must improve your listening skills, no?" I clenched my hands into fists. "There can only be one winning team, that is always the outcome of the final zone. So, we will stay a step ahead and take them out as we go. I'm sure the others all agree, yes?"

There was no answer from Dylan, he seemed to be struggling to keep calm. A muscle pulsed like a beacon in his cheek. I didn't know what triggered a werewolf, but they did have a reputation for violence. The catalyst for the separation was supposedly blamed on them after a particularly gruesome incident years ago.

"That is what they will be planning to do to us," Chris added, as if that settled the matter.

We continued onward, an awkward silence settling between Dylan and me. He walked almost on top of me to the extent I could taste his breath as it condensed as sweat on my skin. It wasn't threatening, but it was unnerving.

"What's your favorite color?" he whispered in my ear.

I jumped, even though his voice was barely a breath. "What?"

"I always knew humans had terrible hearing, it's no wonder you go around shouting all day long," he said. His face widened into a grin, pointed teeth catching the dappled light like piano keys. "Shall I stand closer?"

He was basically on top of me. And he was serious. I just blinked at him. "Orange," I muttered, shaking my head as if that would extinguish the weirdness of the moment.

"That's an odd choice."

I stopped. He sidestepped around me, surprisingly

agile, his shoulder not even glancing mine as he did. I folded my arms and stared at him. It was the stance I always took when confronted. A habit I could never break, even though it was usually followed by my sister pulling the exact same pose and rolling her eyes in mimicry of me.

Dylan nodded and began to walk away.

"Wait! What's yours then?" It felt rude not to ask. I didn't know if he was trying to get to know me or just humans in general. Maybe he wasn't sure what colors we could see with our puny eyes and dull senses. Maybe he was genuinely curious about what colors we appreciated in the world around us.

Turns out I was giving him too much credit, and this wasn't some deep existential question.

"Orange as well," he said, and continued walking.

If you have finally finished your conversation, maybe we can get back to business?

"How nice of you to ask so politely," I muttered, hurrying after Dylan.

The other teams have already begun searching. There is a natural clearing in the center of the jungle which would provide a good place equidistant from all the teams' starting positions where the Vessel of Unity could be.

We should set up surveillance and wait until nearer the end of the time limit to take it from whichever team tries to claim it. That way keeping out of the scheming and fighting.

I relayed the suggestion to the group.

"No, girl. We will get it first and keep it. There can be no risk of it falling into anyone else's hands. Do you understand?"

"Do you even know what it is we're looking for?" I asked.

"This is the first time they have used an object and made the teams locate it, instead of choosing who they will award it to. It will be obvious to those of sharp mind when we do find it. Chris here," she gave him another smile, "will probably recognize it straight away, no?"

Dylan snorted and I shook my head.

"Maybe you should take my annihilator actually, Dylan." I turned to him. "They haven't given you any weapons and you're probably going to be more use than I will be."

"I'll protect you," he whispered. He seemed to be standing very close again and his yellow eyes were fixed on my face.

No one had ever said those words to me before, least of all a stranger. "Erm ... well ... sure," I said. "I didn't mean ... erm, well, that's not what I was asking..." What was wrong with me? Why was he making me so nervous? I swallowed and tried again. "I think you had better concentrate on yourself first."

This time the wind slapped me in the face with a burst of laughter. "He doesn't need any weapons, girl. He knows exactly what he was born to do and how best to use his talents. Don't you, wolf? Yes?"

He snarled again, auburn hair bristling like flames as he stepped toward her.

"Time to go! Chris, are you ready to lead us?" She made a graceful sweeping gesture with her flowing hands and sprang off in the lead into the dense jungle.

Grudgingly I followed behind them, Dylan stuck to my heels.

The scarlet macaw shrieked and soared through the canopy above us, her shadow blending with the sun-dappled floor.

NK BROWN

Chapter Seven

"Why is it getting hotter?" I mumbled as I brushed more sweat off my sticky forehead. My glove was dripping wet, and I removed it. The other one was stuck fast, trapping my hand inside the boiling fabric.

It is the jungle.

"Funny!" I grumbled. "There's not even any direct sun. Where is the heat coming from?"

"You need to stop talking to it," Chris said from in front, not even bothering to turn around. "Don't trust anything you can't see. It's probably a deception sent to confuse you and separate you from the team."

"It's not an '*it*'," I snapped, wiping more sweat from my back, "*they* is the correct pronoun. Don't you know this stuff, working for the government? I would have thought it would be day one of your training." I put on my most superior sounding voice. "How to identify the different beings correctly so I don't sound like a complete moron."

Dylan chuckled quietly from behind me.

Then, because I just couldn't help myself, "Aren't you hot in those trousers?"

The black leather was glistening with sweat and there was a quiet squeaking as he walked.

Pixie turned around with a shimmer of her long hair and narrowed her eyes at me. The purple irises pulsed black before returning to the original shades of violet.

"Ouch!"

A stabbing pain struck my lower back, closely followed by an itching which prickled and burned as the sweat poured over it. I reached back to scratch at it and instantly yanked my hand away, contacting something red-hot. An acrid, burning smell reached my nostrils and I tentatively reached around again using the glove as protection and grabbed the smoldering handle of the annihilator. I wrenched it out of my waistband, feeling a tearing as the skin ripped off my lower back with it. I held it up with my fingertips, gaping in horror at the layer of charred flesh attached to the metal barrel.

"Be careful of her," Dylan snarled from behind me.

The macaw shrieked again and flew off. I expected the sharp hooked beak to come and clean off the flesh, but instead she disappeared. The soft fluttering of wings fanned the humid air around me a few moments later, offering no relief against the heat, and she dropped a large thorn covered leaf into my gloved hand. The green inch long spikes were camouflaged against its rough surface and I turned back to Dylan confused. He grabbed it from me, unconcerned as the thorns speared into his flesh and tore it open.

"Put out your hand." He was no longer whispering, the words forced out from gritted teeth as his control waned.

He squeezed a foul-smelling green slime onto my palm and sighing heavily in anticipation, I smeared it onto my burned back. The burn was worse. The singed odor doubled in the air as white-hot pokers stabbed at me. I tried to wipe it off, but Dylan grabbed my arms. His long fingers clamped around my arms like a vice. Too tight. Too constrictive.

"Stay still!" he growled.

I tried to obey, but my body was writhing and bending as I squirmed away from the burning. He bent down, face inches from mine and snarled. There was fire in his eyes and the sharp points of his canine teeth protruded from his strained mouth. My stomach inverted and my heart pounded in my chest. It was too much. Too surreal.

As the sap started to seep into my raw skin, bringing with it the blissful release of pain, I burst into hysterical laughter. Tears ran down my face and my stomach muscles ached as my body contorted. Dylan stepped back from me with a look caught somewhere between horror and amusement on his face. I hiccupped loudly, interrupting the sob-infused bursts of hysteria and a growl of laughter joined me. I brushed the tears from my face, using the remaining gloved hand to absorb them. As I glanced up at him another hiccup broke free and both of us descended into peals of laughter.

"Try and be quiet, this is not a game, yes?" Pixie's voice scolded from in front, swirling around with the wind.

"You started it," I mumbled, and Dylan's grin widened.

We set off after them again, forcing aside bushy ferns and hopping over large roots and patches of slippery moss. I felt much lighter as I trotted along, Dylan striding next to me.

Turning to him again, I said in a whisper, "Do you think now is a good time to ask about that poultice for my shoulder?"

He raised his eyebrows in response.

"Okay, well maybe we can use some more of the green fire slime." I squinted into the green canopy. "Where's Amura?"

"She is probably scouting the way," Dylan whispered, but there was an edge of doubt in his voice.

As soon as my eyes left the floor I instantly caught against a root and stumbled. Dylan grabbed me, one hand on my arm and the other around my waist. I mumbled a thank you and cursed the fiery blush spreading over my cheeks. He seemed reluctant to let go, his fingers tracing every inch of my skin before releasing.

We both stopped, our breaths faster than they ought to be. A flash of color caught my eye, and I scanned the treetops looking for the source, Dylan doing the same. Directly above us were the lurid tones of a blue jay. It sat immobilized, garishly bright against the khaki-colored background. As our eyes fell on him, he screamed a cackling laugh and shot off, skimming and weaving through the dense branches.

"I'm not crazy. That's not a normal jungle bird, right?"

"Right," he whispered.

"How long has it been spying on us?"

He shrugged.

Pixie flitted back over to us, hands on hips as she scrutinized Dylan. "You don't know where Amura is? You had better start paying more attention, wolf. You have the best senses of any of us, so use them, yes?"

"It's not his fault!" I shot back.

"No, it's probably yours," said Chris, coming back to join us. "Amura probably went to find a better team, with others less insufferable than you."

I rolled my eyes at him. "None of this is helpful. We need to find her." I turned to Dylan who still had Pixie fixed in his stare and nudged him gently, but he didn't respond, so I pushed him harder. "Dylan!"

A flash of rage forked like lightning in his eyes, his jaw set, face contorted as he turned his anger toward me instead.

A chill plunged down my spine and I stepped back. "Erm, okay … well…"

As the distance widened between us, he frowned, head tilting and face softening. The tug of guilt slumped his shoulders.

I cleared my throat. "Can you find her?"

He snorted. "Of course."

He stomped off ahead with Pixie flitting around him. Chris followed closely, and I went last, sneaking glances up at the canopy as I went.

Pixie threw out a delicate hand in front, stopping Chris in his tracks and I halted just behind. Dylan came back a few steps and moved in front of me, his bulky torso blocking my view leaving me no choice but to peer around him.

On the narrow trail up ahead, feet barely making a dent upon a patch of springy green moss, there was another being. He looked almost identical to Pixie, ever-changing hues of purple outlining strange black pupils, shimmering hair rippling in long waves down his back. He wore a blue necklace of seashells across his swan-like neck, rather than the red leaves she had, and when he spoke his voice trickled like bubbling water.

"Friends," he began, "I've come to propose a trade."

NK BROWN

Chapter Eight

It was eerily quiet. All the buzzing and throbbing life around me ceased. Even the wind had died. Pixie was as still as I had ever seen her. Tension radiated through her stiff back and shoulders, usually so supple and graceful. She made a small gusting motion with her hand, and the other pixie continued.

"As a team, we have decided that we all may fare better if we swapped humans." The words were cooling as they trickled over my sweat-soaked skin. Tempting. His violet eyes flashed in my direction. "A straight swap, blue girl for red."

"Sure."

"No."

Chris and Dylan answered in unison, the latter a snarl.

"Erm, no, thanks," I added.

"Well, we have something else to sweeten the deal." He pulled out a long red tail feather, seemingly out of thin air. "Swap the girls and you can have the bird. You can't go very far without her."

"That's not proof he has her," I whispered, "it's only a feather."

"It is her feather," Dylan replied as his nose twitched.

"Probably better to not risk it," Chris said. "Trades are allowed if all parties agree. We could probably get an upgrade."

"Why do you want *this* girl?" Pixie asked, unable to hide the skepticism in her voice.

"She has a talent we are lacking," came the gentle reply.

Chris turned his head and eyed me again as if he

had missed something the first time around. I glared back at him.

The wind was back, stronger and more forceful than before. "I think we will keep the girl for a little longer, no?" She still held her hand high, as if she had forgotten it belonged to her body. "Also, the half-blood seems to have become unexplainably attached to her."

I cursed the blush prickling the skin of my chest and neck again. As much as I disliked her, she was right. It was unexplainable.

With a terse nod of his head and a momentary black flash of his eyes, he turned and flowed away, immediately disappearing into the dense jungle.

"Werewolf," Pixie turned to Dylan, "you are I are going to follow him and get Amura back. You still have the scent, yes?"

He nodded, his nostrils flaring as a look of disgust washed over his face.

"You two are going to find somewhere to hide until we come back. You think you can do that, girl, without getting into trouble, yes?"

"I'll make sure she behaves," Chris said, with a wink at me.

I mimed gagging and Dylan bared his teeth quietly. With a reluctant look back at me, Dylan padded forward, and he and Pixie disappeared into the dense jungle. When he left my side, it was as if I had been pushed out of a warm log cabin and into the wilderness. Suddenly naked and exposed to not only the elements but every creature in the realm.

Smothering the feeling, I crossed my arms again and turned back to Chris. "What's the point of hiding?" I asked. "If they can find us again then every other stinking creature in this place can as well."

"I really have no idea what he sees in you."

I blinked in surprise. "Right, okay, well, that's insulting. Maybe we should just wait in silence, no?" I raised my voice at the end and twirled my hand in as close to an intimation my clumsy human form could muster.

He shook his head and continued, "There are reports of werewolves that fall for humans, but it doesn't happen that often. They say they were attracted by a particular smell or defining feature, but in your case..." he trailed off, looking me up and down slowly, "it really does not make any sense."

"I really don't know what you are talking about. Besides, aren't you the one who said he is supposed to be protecting us?"

"Yes, exactly. Protecting both of us."

He began to move off along the trail and my foot suddenly shot out, tripping him. He fell forward heavily, hands slamming against a boulder to break his fall. He glared at me, and I shrugged.

"It really doesn't make any sense. My foot just..." I trailed off looking him up and down slowly, unable to stop the grin sliding across my face.

We walked in silence for a long while. Chris was silently seething, and the thought cheered me up slightly. I kept scanning the tree line above for any animals, but saw no one. Out of the corner of my eye, movement kept snagging my attention but every time I looked, it turned out to be just a vibrant plant, shimmering in the heat.

Rustling sounded, barely a foot away in the dense jungle. I froze, my heart slamming against my ribs, expecting to be thrown down and trapped under razor-sharp pincers once again. But it was only the rapid closing of a leaf I'd brushed past, its sticky petals snagging on my clothes and triggering the chain reaction of the rest of the bush.

The sweat continued to pour off me and the familiar dryness crept into my mouth. Eventually, Chris stopped in front and opened the pack, handing me my canteen. I drank gratefully, the water warm, but still refreshing for my parched mouth.

"How could anyone trap a shapeshifter anyway?" I asked between sips.

"It's not difficult. You just need fresh blood. Human blood."

There was a silence as I considered this.

"You remind me of my sister," he said, taking my canteen away from me before I was finished.

I didn't feel a compliment coming on, so I remained quiet.

"She would always rebel against authority, chose her own rules to follow, for no reason other than to be different, other than to create some excitement."

"How is that like me?"

He held up a hand and I shook my head at him.

"Listen, the truth is," he lowered his voice, "that if we lose and somehow aren't killed then the government will take us. They don't publicize what happens, although the general consensus is that everyone dies during the experiment and only the winners are ever freed. But I've seen the holding cells." He paused, his brown eyes intent on mine. "And I've heard the reasoning for what they do next. They talk about furthering their 'research' and about finding out on a genetic level why we can't interact together. No one ever hears from those test subjects again. Understand?"

I nodded.

"I'd rather be killed in here," he added.

We both fell silent as his words hung in the air.

Like my father, I thought.

What did I want? To die? To survive? To be

instrumental in creating this elusive 'unity'? I wanted the unity experiment to be a success, I always have. I wanted it even more since my father died trying to forge the path. But it's one thing to think about making a difference, to talk idly about being part of progress, and it's far easier to want it from a distance. Easier to say you strive for peace, especially when people are watching, judging, basing their opinion of you on the words pouring from your mouth. All the while you are safely tucked away at home and what's happening is in no way directly affecting you.

Maybe it's a good thing I'm here and being forced into action, rather than withering away at home. I'm not a hero and I'm nobody's savior, but Chris is wrong. This is not where I wanted to die.

"Is it still with you?" Chris asked, changing the subject.

"Is what still with me?"

"The spirit."

"Oh." For some unknown reason I looked up at the sky and then around as if the spirit would suddenly materialize. "They've been quiet, so actually I think maybe they went with the others."

"Well, you need to be careful. Find out exactly what kind of spirit it is. From what I've seen so far, you are obviously the gullible type."

I glared at him.

He shrugged in response. "We might not get along, but if we both want to survive this thing you've got to start being more careful. Remember the spirits often have nothing to lose and have their own agenda. I've seen it many times over the years. As they have no representation in government anymore, many just want to enact revenge on the humans who took that right away."

A soft moaning filtered through the trees, followed by a ripping sound like the tearing of a canvas tent. I glanced at him and then moved in the direction of the noise.

He grabbed my elbow and hissed at me, "What are you doing?"

Ignoring him, I shook him off my arm and crept along, gently pushing aside velvety soft ferns, my feet silent on the thick moss. Crouching down just before a small clearing, I peered through the narrow fronds.

A young girl was lying on her back, golden hair fanned around her. She was wearing bright blue gloves, which hung limply by her sides. Her whole body was slack, providing no resistance to the figure above.

A shape loomed over her, hair so black it appeared blue in the dappled light. A soft sucking noise floated across, reminding me of a blackbird tugging out thin elastic worms from the wet earth. The worms would stick slightly, coiled tightly in their protected home, then with a jerk, were whipped free and devoured.

Bile burned in the back of my throat as my stomach churned. Chris watched next to me, face frozen in horror.

"We've found the girl from the blue team," I whispered, my voice cracking.

Chapter Nine

I reached back for the annihilator wrapped in my spare glove and slowly brought it up and into view. It was still warm from Pixie's burning charm despite the protective fabric layer. Aiming the square nozzle between the green fingers of the fern, I gently pressed the trigger. The propulsion knocked me back as the muzzle jerked violently upward. Crackling filled the air, and the smell of singed flesh coated my nostrils.

The girl in the blue gloves vanished, but the jet-black eyes of the shapeshifter were now fixed on me. There was an emptiness in the dark expression, but swirling below it, a seething hatred.

Too slowly I raised the sleek metal again, but before I could fire, it was wrenched out of my hands, the trigger depressing. Another crack fired and the huge walking-tree whose stilt-like roots we had just crawled past vanished, a thick plume of grey smoke winding into the dense air in its place. I slammed backward, the dense foliage cushioning my fall, preventing my spine from shattering like glass.

He was on top of me. Pale lips stretched wide over blood-stained fangs. There was something caught in his teeth. The pink sheen of a mucosal layer. His rancid breath inched closer, the dangling object suspended millimeters from my face. My stomach contracted as I heaved up acidic bile, managing to turn my head enough so that it spewed to the side and splattered on the floor. There was a moment of confusion as the shapeshifter pulled away, nose twitching before a spear was rammed into his head.

The weight lifted from my body, and I rolled to my side, coughing and gagging. Wiping my mouth on my one good sleeve, I groaned, pushing myself onto an elbow. Chris was standing off to the side, panting heavily.

A small blue jay lay inert on the shady floor. Its bottomless black eyes open. A razor-sharp spear of wood stuck out of its head, the roughly torn handle protruding from the other side. The only blood to be seen was a dried smear on its pointed beak and a pink sliver of ingesta wedged between the grooves of its jaw.

"Next time," Chris panted, "try killing the vampire first."

I collapsed back on the soft ground and lay still. My stomach was still churning, and the smell of charred flesh and smoke hung heavily in the air. Blinking slowly, the surrounding trees swam in and out of focus.

A flash of sunlight emanated from a smoky leaf but when I fixed my pupils on the spot it faded back to green. From the corner of my eye another flash came, and I swiveled my gaze, but again, nothing but foliage filled my vision.

Slowly my mind slotted the clues into place.

The flash returned, golden against the monotone backdrop and I threw myself at Chris's legs, dragging him to the floor. He landed heavily, palms smacking into the ground as the pulse whipped over his head, the hum of electricity singing in our ears. Another huge tree exploded. The thick black cloud joining the charred remains of its decades old friend.

On hands and knees, we crawled back into the deep bushes as a human voice rang out clear through the trees. "Come on out now, children," the woman cooed, "let's get this over with."

Where was my weapon? The red glove that housed my annihilator was nowhere to be seen. Completely unarmed and still trembling, I glanced over at

Chris. His annihilator was raised and ready, a determined look in his sharp eyes.

From across the small clearing another figure emerged. A young boy, barely twelve years old, was carrying a transparent cage. He wore golden gloves and held it by a small invisible handle on the top, carelessly letting it swing around like a watch on a chain. Inside the cage, a robin with a blood-red breast slid around. Black talons screeched over the smooth floor as she tried to find purchase before being slammed against the invisible walls.

The boy paused, barely a foot out of the protection of the enveloping leaves and another figure emerged. A vast, broad chest, muscles perfectly chiseled against the golden fur, supported a huge head. It was framed by a halo of chocolate covered mane and completed by long, dangerous white fangs. Its large mouth gaped, and it roared. All the flora within reach bent backward by the force and I grimaced as the sound ricocheted around in my head.

Another deep growl answered from behind us, this one bringing a small sigh of gratitude to my lips. The werewolf leapt out and into the clearing, auburn fur smoldering in the sunlight.

The wind started blowing around us again. It whispered, "One of you get the cage."

Chris held his annihilator steady, finger feather-light over the trigger as he cut his eyes at me. I nodded back. It had to be me. I sucked in a deep breath and raised myself to a crouching position, ready to bolt. Nausea hollowed out my limbs and made the clearing shimmer at the edges of my vision, but adrenaline pumped through my bloodstream, filling my weakness. I was ready.

The lion circled, huge feet padding softly on the ground, barely making a dent. Dylan snarled, hackles raised, matching it step for step. I had to be quick. I couldn't let Dylan get hurt. The wind picked up, first as a warm breeze rustling the leaves before it accelerated, howling through the trees.

With a splintering crack, a large black shadow raced toward the clearing and the boy. He dived to the side of the falling tree, but a branch slashed down his side, tearing open a gaping red hole. His gloved fingers released the handle and the cage plummeted to the ground.

I sprang out of the fern and sprinted directly across the clearing. The lion's black eyes shone in predatory excitement as it shifted focus from the werewolf and onto its prey. Onto me. The leaves and mulch from the floor whipped up around me as I ran, blinding the lion as it roared in frustration. The vicious swipe of Dylan's claws connected deeply with its flesh as I tore past.

I grabbed at the cage, unable to find the handle in my panic and the slippery curved surfaces spun around in my arms. Hugging it tightly to my chest, I carried on running blindly into the forest. My feet pounded the sparse trail, eyes frantically straining for any curling roots. I kept focused straight ahead, not daring to risk turning around.

I only slowed when my lungs screamed in protest and a fiery pain burned across my chest. Spinning in a tight circle, I strained to listen over the sound of my heavy breathing. No one seemed to be following. Unwrapping my arms, I peered down at Amura. Her feathers were fluffed and broken and there was a haughty look of contempt in her beady eyes.

"Sorry," I muttered.

I ran my hands over the smooth surfaces, looking for a hinge, a door, anything. It was as perfect as a sheet of ice. I thought about throwing it against a tree but the murderous look in the black eyes as I glanced down at her stopped me.

It opens by blood.

Of course, it does.

"Welcome back," I said, glancing around into the empty air. "Where were you?"

There was no answering reply, so I turned my attention back to the cage. I picked wimpily at the fragile scab over my shoulder. The muscle underneath burned, and needles of pain shot down my arm as my skin clung tightly onto its protective barrier. Gritting my teeth, I pulled harder and ripped the crust away. Fresh blood trickled down my skin, mixing with the mud and moss and all the other stains I had accumulated over the past few hours. I put the cage on the floor and let the disgusting mixture drip slowly onto it, covering the clear walls.

Impatiently, I waited. Sweat joined the blood and dripped onto the cage. Nothing seemed to be happening. I reached down and smeared the warm, sticky concoction like paint over a canvas and gradually the golden lines of a small door appeared. I pressed down on it and with a small click, it swung open, and a burst of angry red and brown feathers exploded out. She transformed in front of me and stood with translucent hands on slim hips, whilst her eyes blazed like her flame-red hair.

Nothing came out when I opened my mouth.

"Not the treatment I am used to." Her usual melodic voice trilled sharply.

She turned on her heel and was about to stalk away, but I reached out and gently touched her arm. She spun around, wrenching it from me and loomed, face inches from mine.

My resolve faltered. My mouth had gone dry

again and my tongue seemed stuck, unable to form any coherent words. "Erm, well, I…" I cleared my throat and tried again. "I'm sorry."

Her head cocked slightly, the short spikes of hair falling to the side.

"We were looking for you. Well, Pixie and Dylan was. Erm, I mean were. Chris and I were told to stay put. We thought the blue team had you but…"

She continued to stare at me.

"Are you okay, though?" I persisted. "Can I do anything for you? Are you injured?" I had no idea how to comfort a shapeshifter.

Her face softened slightly and a look of surprise, strongly mixed with incredulity, raised her perfectly shaped eyebrows. "Can you do anything for me?" A squawk of laughter burst from her lips, and I started at the sound, stepping back reflexively. "No, human. But what is that saying you have?" She considered a moment. "It's the thought that counts."

"So, what happened?"

If she breathed, she would've sighed in defeat. I waited expectantly.

"I think, human," she paused briefly, "you do not understand the importance of this experiment. Your government keeps you secluded from the other beings— they say for your own safety. What they don't tell you is the conditions in which the marginalization has forced *us* to live. We are on the brink of extinction. Isolated and starving. Hemmed into far deserted corners of the world whilst we watch those we care about fade away. I doubt you have ever suffered from a lack of freedom in your life?"

I didn't answer. She was right. We all lived, on the whole, the way we wanted. There were areas that were out of bounds of course. And as the tension between the beings increased, the range we were able to inhabit decreased. But the only impact this had on my life was when our usual family vacation spot had been changed.

"So, human, my lack of control which allowed the gold team to trap me is exactly the kind of behavior that is not supposed to happen. I am supposed to be above those base urges. The goal of this experiment should not be forgotten."

"It's not your fault, Amura."

"The fault only lies with me." She folded her arms across her chest. "Anyway, for releasing me from the cage, I now owe *you*."

"No, it's okay. You don't owe me anything. We are supposed to be a team."

She didn't look convinced.

"Do you know why the gold team wanted you?"

She nodded. "They thought that by capturing me they could draw the entire red team in. They were simultaneously keeping me from joining in the inevitable fight and wiping out a whole team of competitors."

"But why us?"

"Because you were given the Vessel of Unity at the start of the experiment."

I blinked at her. "No, I wasn't."

"It was in the backpack. That information was given to the gold team in their instructions."

I cast my mind back. I had glanced in briefly and seen only basic supplies before Chris took it from me.

"Are you sure?" I asked.

"Well, when we get back to the team we can check."

I nodded. "So, it was just a stray feather the blue team had. They must have seen the gold team trap you and think they could use the information to blackmail us for their trade."

"Hmm, yes." She considered this for a moment. "So, I see that our team decided to keep you, instead of trading for me?"

I looked away. "I mean, not really. Chris wanted to swap me right away, so…"

"Hmm."

Amura unfolded her arms and stretched them above her head with an audible crack. She gave a satisfied smile before jumping into the air. The macaw started to fly back the way we had come, before veering back toward me. She clipped my mangled shoulder with her outstretched wing feathers. The touch somewhere between a playful push from a sibling and the bone-shattering crack of a quarterback. She squawked a burst of laughter.

Grimacing, I jogged after her.

Chapter Ten

We hadn't gone far when she zoomed off into the trees again and I lost sight of the long scarlet feathers.

"Amura, wait!"

The only response was a distant croaking of a bullfrog and some tittering from a hoard of nearby insects. My previous trail through the jungle was slowly disappearing as the rubbery stems straightened themselves and my footprints were absorbed by the rich floor. I had no sense of direction, being unable to locate the sun and no intention of climbing one of the trees for a better view.

The spirit wasn't offering any helpful advice either. They seemed to just pop in and out whenever they felt like it. Sighing, I attempted to walk in as straight a line as possible. A quiet bubbling sound wafted across from nearby, bringing with it the rancid smell of sulphur. I stopped and looked around. As quick as it had come, the smell disappeared, and the normal sounds of life resumed. Then another noise reached me like the wet smacking of a frog's lips, this time closer and louder.

I glanced around again, eyes darting between the shadows, trying to locate the disturbance. A large hand clamped down on my mouth and another wrapped around my chest dragging me backward. The tendrils of a large fern grabbed at my clothes, trying in vain to help. I kicked out but met nothing but damp air. I tried to scream but my voice was muffled, forced back down into my lungs by the foreign hand. I had a brief glimmer of hope that at least it was a human who had me and not some hideous jungle creature.

I was jerked upright, and my feet scrabbled to find the floor. He still held me, uncomfortably tight and unyielding. The sounds of my terrified breathing filled the air as I tried to inflate my lungs using the narrow passageways of just my flaring nostrils. A swamp gurgled a few feet away, the brown surface almost camouflaged with the jungle floor. The smell slunk over, rising bile in my throat.

"Are you out here all alone, my dear?" The voice was low and silky and eerily familiar. Had I heard it on the plane? My heart pounded faster. "Such a shame they turned down the trade. We could have had so much fun together."

Another voice joined in, almost whining with excitement. "Let her go, it's my turn."

The vice around me didn't loosen. The second voice crept closer, and I found myself looking up into wide, shining, almond shaped eyes. A sneer was stretched tight across his tanned face, shards of electric blue running through his textured hair. The distance closed between us, and I struggled against the muscular body holding me. He pressed his moist nose against the bounding pulse in my neck and inhaled deeply, dragging his face up and over my skin.

The hand around my mouth loosened and I whipped my head away, sucking in air. The pressure around my chest disappeared as the arm around me fell limp. I pushed it roughly away, taking my weight on shaking legs.

The werewolf froze in front of me, confusion lining his hard face. He stared over my shoulder at the glassy-eyed expression of the man who had grabbed me, now standing as still and harmless as a doll. His nose sniffed the air, eyes darting over his pliable form.

"He's been possessed." The words trickled over to

me. The pixie with the blue shell necklace had appeared from nowhere. He stood quietly, his slim frame blocking the only opening between the densely packed ferns. A ripple of energy disturbed the calm air around him like concentric circles radiating from a stone hurled into a puddle. "Did you do this?" he asked me.

Lying seemed like the better option here. I nodded. The werewolf flared his nostrils again and backed away until his feet hovered at the edge of the bubbling mud, his low whine filling the clearing.

The pixie fixed his gaze on the stupefied man. I stepped away and pressed back against a tree, glad of the increased distance between myself and all of them. The rippling around the pixie increased in intensity, his outline now a blur. A small wrinkle formed between his eyebrows whilst his lips shaped unheard words.

I hovered nervously at the edge of his vision, time crawling by.

Eventually, the wrinkle smoothed out on his forehead and his eyes slid toward me. "I cannot undo it. You must release him, girl."

I glanced at the man. Even if I had any idea what had happened to him, it would be stupid to set him free again. A bead of sweat trickled down his shaved head, tracing the outline of the jailhouse tattoo which spread from his jagged ear down his muscular neck and disappeared beneath a t-shirt stretched too tight. He must have been the released prisoner from the plane. Probably never imagined this turn of events.

As if reading my thoughts, the pixie continued, "We mean you no harm. We came in peace to offer a trade. Our shapeshifter has observed your interaction with the spirit on your team and ours is lacking anyone with those abilities." His voice took on a persuasive edge, the tinkling sound almost hypnotic. "Without a medium we are without any guidelines. We are without any input or structure from the Human Government running the experiment. It is almost as if they want us to fail." He gave a small bubbling laugh before sobering. "My poor teammates were very stressed about this and must be excused for any fright they may have caused you. We all want to forge the unity as much as you, my dear."

He was obviously unaware as to the fate of both their human and shapeshifter teammates. Even with a trade, their time was over.

"Look, I'm sorry. I really can't help you—" I began, but the werewolf cut me off.

"Just leave her and let's go. We may still be able to escape before they find us." He was still standing as far from the possessed man as possible, eyes not leaving the slack face.

An uncomfortable silence filled the clearing as the pixie took a step toward me. My intestines writhed deep within my stomach. The sharp bark of the tree dug into my back as I pressed harder against it.

He took another step closer.

A slender figure dropped down from the tree behind him, spraying the ground with unsettled dew. The air around him rippled with a resounding boom that shook the leaves from the nearby trees sending the figure soaring up and into the forest. I caught a glimpse of flame-red hair being swallowed by the dripping foliage before his purple eyes fixed back on me.

Before I could blink, Amura was on him again. Her body was distinctly human but there was nothing familiar amount her features. The dark eyes were filled with a burning anger, the pale face contorted and haggard. Her sharp teeth bit and slashed as the shriek of the macaw boomed out.

The rippling hair of the pixie swirled around him

in defense, enveloping him like a cyclone. A deafening roar like the pounding of a waterfall erupted from him and she dived inside. The cylinder of water bulged then exploded, showering droplets of icy water all around.

Amura stood in the center, hair spiked up, water running in rivulets down her. She wasn't panting. She wasn't tired. She looked alive. Dangling from her hand was the delicate blue necklace. A dark substance oozed from deep within the seashells and dripped quietly onto the floor.

From the corner of my vision, the ferns rustled faintly as the werewolf bolted.

"Just so you know," I said, "that doesn't count as making us even."

Amura narrowed her eyes at me.

"I wasn't in danger. The blue pixie didn't want to hurt me, he just wanted me to help them."

"You were trapped between a werewolf and a pixie. Of course, you were in danger, human."

"Nope," I shook my head. "So, you still owe me."

My grin was answered by an unblinking stare.

"Fine," she said, "kill the human and let's go." She inclined her head in the direction of the man.

"What? Why?" I spluttered. "I'm not doing that. You do it."

I glanced over at him. He still stood dumb, hands limp at his side. The straps of a bright blue backpack dug into his broad shoulders as a trickle of saliva crept down his slack face. I had absolutely no intention of killing him. There was no danger. He was like a lost lamb, alone with foxes.

She considered the request. Then she gave a slight shake of her head. "I don't need to. He's not my type."

We both stood and stared at the helpless man.

"You do it," Amura began again, "or you can

explain to Pixie why you decided to let him live when we get back to the group."

Urgh. I could almost hear the conversation now. The mock disappointed tone that didn't even try to hide the condescension. The sparkle in her eyes as she laid into me in front of the group for not following her directions.

"I never agreed to kill anyone," I said.

"Good luck telling her that, human."

The swamp behind us bubbled. Every burst wafted the sulphur smell over to us. I wrinkled my nose in protest, wanting to leave as quickly as possible.

"We can't leave him here like this, though," I said.

"So, kill him. Before something else does."

We stood again in silence as the jungle resumed its life around us, unconcerned by our indecision.

"I'll do it myself."

We both stared at the vacant face of the man whose mouth was working mechanically, the silky voice oozing out. His hand reached down to a holster on his waist. I expected to see the shiny handle of an annihilator tucked away in there, but he pulled out an exquisitely carved wooden handle. A long, curved blade flashed in a stray ray of sunlight. I had a moment of jealousy that he had been bestowed such a weapon. Then he carved the blade along his throat and soundlessly slumped to the floor.

Amura's eyes flashed as the sweet scent of blood drifted over to us. She leapt into the air and the wailing screech of the macaw sounded from the trees high above.

The man on the floor groaned, murmuring unintelligible words. His eyes were darting around, his hands groping at his neck. Kneeling next to him, I patted him awkwardly on his chest.

"Just stay calm," I whispered.

His hand stopped fumbling at his neck and gripped my arm. His eyes found mine. He sucked in a strained breath and drew me closer. My body tensed, straining to keep a distance between us but still wanting to comfort him.

"I don't regret a second," he wheezed. "I was never going to go back." He swallowed, blinking slowly as he drew another long breath. "Don't ever let them catch you, girl."

I wished that whatever had possessed him had stuck around, so that at least he didn't have to be conscious for this part.

A shadow of a smile was on his lips as he said, "Now I'm going to come back and haunt the lot of them."

His fingers loosened around my arm and his chest stilled as his eyes glazed over once more. This time for good.

NK BROWN

Chapter Eleven

The clearing appeared much larger when I reached it again. There were a few more smoking stumps and all the vegetation in a wide circle lay flattened. The huge form of the lion was sprawled in the middle, golden hair completely still with not even a breath of the wind disturbing its peace.

Dylan paced back and forth in front of the lion, fists clenched and jaw tight. When his eyes fell on me, he strode across the trampled ground and halted, barely inches away. The heat pulsed from him, and his familiar scent of cinnamon mixed now with blood and smoke enveloped me.

I leaned in closer, curious and surprised. His honey eyes up close were all one color. No flecks, no shades, just intense yellow. Warmth tingled through me, my lips parting just a breath.

It slowly dawned on me that he was looking at me like prey. His face was tense and posture threatening as he loomed over me. I backed up. I'd seriously misread the situation. Had our tentative friendship been fractured by my disappearance? Or maybe he'd never liked me, he was just doing his job as Chris said.

Amura reappeared with two large spiny leaves and dropped them on the floor. The motion acted as a distraction, and Dylan seemed to soften again. The tension leaving his body like a sigh of relief. I lowered my gaze, my attention falling to a long bloody gash down his strong arm. He picked one up and ripped it open.

"Let me help." I gingerly took the leaf, making sure to avoid the inch long thorns and raised it to his arm. "Let's see how still you stay, tough guy," I mumbled, as the long strings of green sap trickled down his arm.

His lips twitched in a half smile, and he stayed perfectly still. Inwardly cursing him, I reached for the other half of the leaf. The gash in his arm was deep, muscle and tendons exposed by the lion's jagged claws. If it had been someone smaller the arm would have been completely severed. The sap oozed in, plugging the gaping wound.

"I was worried about you," he whispered.

My heart lurched, beating so unnecessarily loud that he would probably be able to hear it. I kept my gaze on his arm as I tended to the wound, but could feel his eyes watching intently, sense that he still had something he wanted to say.

"Where the hell have you been and where is that spirit?" Chris suddenly appeared, stepping into the space between Dylan and me.

I blinked in surprise at his attitude. "Well, I don't know. I have no control over the commun—"

"Don't talk to her like that." Dylan pushed back in front, growling, his hands balled into fists.

"Oh." I put my hand lightly on his arm and eased him back. "No, it's okay. Erm…"

The macaw landed on the ground and Amura stretched up and out of the small body. She raised her arms above her head, cracking her shoulders and rotating her neck. "Easy, humans," she said. "The last thing we need is for you two to kill each other." She gave a small laugh, as if the notion was ludicrous.

Pixie flitted over and joined us, the wind probing as it gusted around us. She looked at Amura a beat longer than was normal whilst Amura's brows furrowed.

"Well, if she is a medium, that would explain many things, no? For starters, why the blue team wanted her in the first place. I, myself, could think of absolutely no reasons."

"You do not have permission to delve into my mind!" Amura spat at her.

"It does, I suppose," Pixie continued, ignoring her, "make you slightly less dull, girl, no?"

"Look," I said, "I have absolutely no idea what any of you are talking about. The only supernatural being that has ever contacted me is the spirit and that is because they said my mind was 'the easiest to access'." I refrained from saying the word 'empty', as I knew Chris would never let that go. "Also, if I were a medium, I would have done far better things with my life. I could've summoned an army of the dead to rescue me from this hell hole or contacted my long dead father to ask for tips on how to deal with beings like you."

Chris held up his hand to silence me. "Let's just say that this is true," he said, "and I don't know why you are getting so worked up about it. But if you have undiscovered talents, then they are going to come in very useful later on in zone three, in the Chasm."

"What's in zone three?" I asked, distracted. "And how do you know about it?"

"It also explains, Chris," added Pixie with a smirk at me, "why the spirit is contacting the girl and not you."

They shared a nod of understanding as if all the mysteries of the world had suddenly been explained and I rolled my eyes at them.

"How do you know what is coming up?" I asked again.

"As I have already told you, *Anna,*" somehow, he managed to infuse even my name with condescension, "I held a position of power within the government and thus am very useful to this team."

"Jealous, more like," Dylan growled.

I bit back a snort of laughter as Chris continued.

"What you conveniently missed, whilst the gold

team was attacking us, was that they now have the Vessel of Unity. It was in the backpack. We need to get it back and there are two of their team unaccounted for. So, I'm going to ask you again, summon the spirit or whatever it is you do, and make it do its job so we can all get the hell out of here."

Tell him the gold werewolf has slunk off somewhere to hide.

Tell him the gold pixie is one and half hours due north.

Then tell him to go fuck himself.

I repeated the first two sentences, not wanting the situation to escalate further.

"Girl, go and find your weapon. You are next to useless without it, yes?" Pixie's soft voice returned as a light breeze entered the clearing. "The rest of us need to discuss how to find the remainder of the gold team."

The wind seemed to gently push us all apart and then she appeared in the center, hair shimmering and face serious. She flicked her hand at me in an 'off you go' gesture. I snorted an irritated breath out of my nose and slunk off across the clearing, back to where Chris and I had crouched down between the ferns, which now seemed like hours ago.

Scanning the ground, I pushed aside plants and even glanced into the low hanging branches, looking for any glimpse of the red glove or black metal. At the far end of the open space the others were arguing again, their voices not carrying far enough for me to hear. Pixie was still between Dylan and Chris, with Amura standing to one side with arms tightly folded, choosing to stay out of the disagreement.

Go further down the trail and then turn right where it branches. Follow the thin stream and you'll find what you are looking for. Go quietly whilst they are distracted.

I glanced back again. They were all looking the other way—even the beady eyes of Amura were focused on something in the distance, unseen through the thick vegetation, so I followed the instructions and crept off down the winding trail.

My feet splashed lightly in the small trickle of water running along the floor. The stream was warm, and I cupped some in my hands and drank. It was welcome to my parched mouth, and I splashed some on my face, trying to wash away some of the filth laying thick upon me.

Up ahead there was a cluster of tall walking trees. Their thin, twisted legs formed a small village of teepees, with a secretive, shady cavern inside each one. Out from between two of the gnarled spindles, two almond shaped eyes emerged. For the first time my trust in the spirit wavered. Frozen, I glanced around nervously, ears straining for the sounds of approaching beings. The eyes blinked slowly, releasing glistening tears, which plunged down into the dark.

"Come closer." The growl was quiet, barely audible. "I have what you want."

My stomach churning, I crept closer. The matted, blonde hair of the werewolf glowed softly in the dark shadows. Her face was wet, body curled up around itself. In her rough hand, lying flat against her palm, was my annihilator.

"There is nothing left for me here or there," her voice was almost a whine, heartbreaking and melancholy. "You humans have a saying, 'you don't know that you're in love until it's gone'. It's not true. It was just told by those who have never felt the true pull of love. Told to ease the feelings of a guilty conscience." More tears trickled from her eyes and ran down her face. "Have you ever fallen in love?"

I shook my head.

"I thought humans fell in and out of love as quickly as puddles form in the rain only to evaporate again in the sun."

I had been in relationships, some just a series of notes passed in school, others more serious. Some boys, some girls, some a platonic connection and others purely physical. I'd never felt the wriggling of butterflies in my stomach when kissing or electricity sparking across fingertips that grazed.

Truthfully, there was never time to let it evolve to that point. Drew took up so much of my attention that things would fizzle. I couldn't hang around after school or purposefully take the long route home just to spend time with whomever I was seeing. If I let Drew out of my sight, he would dash headlong for the woods. Even when he was young enough to believe in the fairytales about gruesome ogres that hunted for stray children or witches that lured in humans with their sweet-scented potions, he still had to see for himself. Then, when he was old enough to know the truth about which beings actually lurked in the forest, he still tried to explore at every opportunity. He seemed determined to find adventure and I was the only one trying to keep him safe.

After a while I stopped trying to socialize. Gave up on finding love. It was easier just to be by myself and concentrate on protecting the family I had left. But a thought emerged unexpected, and it tingled, bristling with possibility—what would it be like to be with Dylan? To have someone protect me for a change?

She gave a heavy sigh, a distant memory tugging the corners of her lips into the shadow of a smile. "If you are in love you know with every fiber of your being. Heart and mind united for eternity. Your eyes can't look anywhere else. You would do anything to protect them. We fall harder than you humans do, and the reward is so much greater. But the pain of loss…

"When we fall in love it's like rain in a lake. We thought we were full, that we had every drop we needed, then we find ourselves expanding, drinking in more. We never knew there was so much room in our hearts and can never go back to how it was. We hold on to every drop and cherish it, making sure to never run dry."

Her confused sentences hung in the air between us, but the meaning was clear. I wanted to reach out to her, to comfort her, but I knew it was more for my sake than hers. She didn't want anything that I could give her.

"We entered together. Sick and tired of having to keep our relationship a secret. It was my idea. My fault. I should have done it by myself." A whine of frustration filled the air. "Of course, they put us on different teams. Who understands their sick logic. If they wanted proof different beings can exist together, they should have just observed our love. Maybe they wanted our teams to work together? Maybe they just wanted a more dramatic ending? Who knows!" Her hand closed around the handle of my annihilator in her palm. "All we wanted was the opportunity to live our lives together. To clear the path for others who share the same destiny."

I remembered the woman on the plane with a pang of guilt. She was probably the only human who had entered the experiment for the right reasons and my only thought so far had been to stay alive. Maybe of winning for the sake of winning and getting out, but not for what the experiment was supposed to stand for.

"How do you know she's…"

"Because I feel it in my soul."

Her fingers loosened around the weapon. She stretched out her hand and I leaned forward and gingerly grasped the handle, easing it from her open palm. I turned to go, but she cried out.

"You have to do it."

My stomach knotted. A lump stuck in my throat. I turned back to her and shook my head.

"If you don't, *they* will."

She meant the governments. I could see the pleading in her eyes, the waver in her voice. I didn't know how they would kill her when they found her or if they would imprison her first. Maybe they would conduct tests like Chris had alluded to. But I did know they wouldn't be kind.

"We'll be together in the afterlife." A resigned smile pulled the corners of her mouth down.

The barrel was shaking, suddenly so heavy in my hand as I raised the square muzzle. The scorch of electricity barely touched my ears this time.

My body absorbed the recoil whilst my heart absorbed her pain.

Chapter Twelve

I stood watching the smoke drift idly upward, wondering if she would find peace in the next life. Wiping my eyes, I started to retrace my steps.

"Can I ask you a question?"

All around me, life was returning to normal. Flies swatted at my face and insects hummed and buzzed in the thick air. The smell of singed flesh faded, leaving only the fresh scent of wet moss.

Yes, you can ask me a question.

"Okay, well," I hesitated, fumbling for the right words, "you possessed that man from the blue team, right? So, what kind of spirit are you? Like, what category do you fall into? Not like, are you good or evil … erm … like are you a spirit or memory or…" I trailed off, the flush rising in my face. "It's just that, erm, Chris said something…" I stopped again, worried I was making things worse.

Silence greeted me. Wonderful. Why did I ask? Why did I need to place them? Stupid Chris. He'd gotten into my head. I backhanded the sweat from my forehead and flicked it onto the bushes.

"Actually, it's okay," I blurted, "I believe in what you are telling me, and I trust you, so you don't need to answer. It doesn't matter."

Unfortunately, that is one of the problems with our world.

There was a pause, silence echoed in my head.

I don't identify wholly with the Spirits, the Memories, the Jinn or any one specific type. I don't straddle two categories. I hold characteristics of all of them and yet are uniquely none.

The itch of embarrassment spread down my neck

and onto my chest like a rash. That is what was wrong with this world. Everyone in a defined category, a specific location, unable to mix or embrace another way of life. I was just as much a part of it as everyone else. I, too, am what was wrong with this world.

You have something else you wanted to ask me as well, I think.

I watched my feet gently disturbing the running water, the flow deftly changing course to continue its route despite the blockage. I did have something else to ask, but I was worried it was going to come across as naïve as well. A small, lime green frog sprung out of the stream and onto a low leaf. The water droplets glistened on its moist skin as it stared at me accusingly. Moving over onto the damp ground next to the water, I took a deep breath.

"I'm sorry for my ignorance, I think I never even tried to understand before. We were told one thing at school, at home, on the radio and I never stopped to think or to doubt it before. Never saw a reason to. My mother told me life after death was nonexistent. I never even tried to open my eyes and look for my father's..." I paused and swallowed, a lump in my throat. "So, I was wondering if you may have ever come across him? I realize you couldn't possibly know everyone out there, but maybe?"

I continued to watch my shoes, my heart thumping noisily in my chest.

No. I'm sorry. Not everyone transitions. Not everyone needs to. Those that are at peace pass straight onto the afterlife. Only those that are unfulfilled or have unresolved business return to the land of the living or become stuck in the Chasm.

"Okay, no problem." I tried and failed miserably at acting nonchalantly, the disappointment thick in my voice.

If he did choose this life, then there is still time for him to find you. Or, for you to find him.

I nodded. They were kind words, but I couldn't believe them. Wherever he was, I hoped he never had to find out how I ended up in the lottery. How I had ended up in the exact same situation as he had. I wasn't sure I was ready to accept the betrayal. I hadn't thought much about it, having been luckily too distracted to really absorb the stabbing pain of deceit. The loss of trust that the severing of our family ties had brought about. How many of them had voted for me? And why?

My hands were trembling again, and the tingle of sobs was starting in my chest. "One last question," I asked, more to distract myself than anything, "why are you here?"

I'm going to tell you a story while we walk. You can make up your own mind, it was a different time back then. We lived in a world with no segregation. All beings able to choose their own path in life with one united government.

But the killings of humans were accelerating.

There started to become a sense of unrest which spread throughout the counties. Small acts of violence, small acts of hate. It was smoldering but kept under control.

A place called the Chasm had been designed but its true use was kept secret from those of us above ground. The government's last ditch attempt at forcing peace.

I raised my daughter alone, for sixteen years it was just the two of us. She was the most perfect creature to ever walk the planet and I would have done anything for her. I made a promise, the very second I gazed into her beautiful sky-blue eyes, that I would never leave her.

When my time came, I would transition. I would choose the life of purgatory, to be trapped in spirit form so that I could look out for her. Make sure she was safe, loved and above all, happy.

She had grown close to the boy next door, Johannes, a werewolf. He came from a lovely family, a mother and father and three siblings. All hard working and dedicated. We kept them apart every full moon but I never had any concerns about him. I could see he was in love with her. Some werewolves fall in love at first sight and they would give their lives for their partner. I knew she was as safe as she could be with him.

For her sixteenth birthday I brought her a silver locket. She had seen it in an antiques shop one day when we were out together and set her heart on it. It was in a beautiful heart shape, the clasp so delicate it was barely holding onto the fine chain. The outside was smooth and so highly polished it was almost reflective. It cost me three months' salary but the look on her face when she opened it, lives with me to this day.

I asked her if she would put herself and Johannes in it and she said she had an idea already and would show me later, when I got back. I had to leave for work that afternoon. There was always an explosion or some sort of crisis occurring in the factories. People being seriously injured or killed, and it was my job to reset the machines so the others could carry on.

When I got home late that afternoon, I went upstairs to see her. We were going to go out together with Johannes's family for dinner and I knew she'd never be ready on time—punctuality was her only vice.

When I got upstairs, her door was slightly ajar. The whole house was silent. I knew deep down something was wrong. I pushed open the door and that was the moment my life ended.

THE UNITY EXPERIMENT

She was lying on her bed, the silver chain embedded in the swollen, purple flesh of her neck. She was almost unrecognizable, but I knew it was her. The locket was in her open palm, pried apart. A picture of me on one side and Johannes on the other.

The security forces evicted the entire family next door and sent them to exile. Johannes was sentenced to death. As I watched him leave the small house next door, he did not fight, he did not protest his innocence. That is why I knew he was not involved.

He died as well that day.

The media storm exploded. They made my baby the figure head for the propaganda. The war between the entities. Her beautiful face was everywhere I turned. I could never escape those sky-blue eyes. The ones that I had failed.

I took my own life barely six months later. I spent many decades searching for her among the spirits of the living. Saw how the world changed, the anger, the resentment, the fear of the unknown. It spread like wildfire. The Unifying Government disbanded and those entities powerful or numerous enough to fight, managed to scrape together new governments.

Negotiations between the entities have been ongoing ever since and the Chasm has been growing exponentially. Lost souls with unfinished business now trapped without an escape, forgotten by the world of the living. The portal was closed with the implosion of the Unified Government and the spirits lost their representation. Now when a being dies, unless they know their duty on earth is done and they pass straight through into the afterlife, they become trapped in the Chasm, unable to go forward or backward.

Zone three involved the Chasm. The spirit needed to find their daughter and I wanted to find my father. I just needed to keep the team together long enough to get there. If the spirit could communicate with me then maybe my father would be able to as well. I had so much I wanted to say to him, so many questions to ask him. He left without a real goodbye, torn away from us, leaving no final sentence of nostalgia to call upon in the depths of night, not even a last word. A flicker of hope trickled into my blood, warming my heart.

The clearing emerged before me, vacant compared to the cramped browns and greens of the dense vegetation I had been trudging through.

"You need to stop wandering off. You're going to get yourself killed and then the rest of us will follow." Chris didn't even look relieved to see me return.

I waved the annihilator in the air sarcastically. Now he smiled, mouth turned down in that way of his.

"One pulse left."

His eyebrows furrowed as he began counting the pulses.

"Gold team werewolf." I didn't elaborate. It still made me feel heavy.

Dylan was beside me instantly. His presence was starting to become familiar. I didn't react, grateful for any act of kindness right now. He would probably prove a useful ally, maybe even a friend. A small part of me whispered that maybe he could be more. His hand was so close to mine, all it would take was a small twitch and our fingers could touch. Perhaps the sparks would fly, sizzling through my skin and charging my body.

But then he seemed to recollect himself and stepped back. Still close enough to be protective, but far enough to allow a gap to form between us.

Chapter Thirteen

We trekked through the rainforest for over an hour. I was surprised that the sweat was still coming, surely my body should have seen the futility of the task and started conserving water by now. The landscape did not change, but I found myself heading down.

My feet slid, unable to find purchase on the increasingly rocky floor. Each large boulder strewn down the gentle slope was covered by delicate but lethal green moss. Landing heavily on my knees for the third time, blood seeping through large fissures in my jeans, I gave up, sitting down and clumsily crab-walking the rest of the way into the small crevasse. I waited at the bottom, rubbing my knees, feeling the damp filtering into my clothes and cursing as it started creeping into my skin too.

There was a fine mist gently rising behind, obscuring the towering trees and ferns. In front was a jagged cave. Its mouth gaped open like an angler fish, one solitary ray of sunlight penetrating the darkness inside.

This was not going to be fun.

Amura landed and changed back into her more human form. Her eyes darted to the gashes on my legs betraying her hunger. She bit her pale lip, it blanched, but no blood seeped out.

"The gold pixie is in the caves. I can lead us to him," she said. Her eyes were still focused on the blood which now spilled down my hands as I tried to staunch the flow.

"This is like your home, no?" Pixie commented, then added, "Where you dreamt of living anyway."

Pixie had an odd way of talking where she would

insert words that made no sense to the rest of us and just served to irritate the speaker. It was like she was intercepting our thoughts. Amura's black eyes left my hands and fixed on her. She chose not to engage and sprang lightly away toward the shadows inside the cave.

Dylan offered me his hand and I hesitated. My fingers were already shaking, sweat lying like a moist film over my palms. My breath was shallow and all I could think about was being trapped. Just the word 'cave' conjured images of tight spaces, crumbling walls and an eternal labyrinth of nightmares.

"I'll just, erm…" I fumbled for any words, my tongue thick in a dry mouth, "stay here and keep a look out."

"There are worse things than being buried alive, no?" Pixie said.

"Comforting," I mumbled, as a mosquito landed stealthily on my exposed skin. I flicked at it lazily and it buzzed away, cursing the loss of a meal.

Don't listen to her, Anna. Stay with Dylan and you will be fine.

When I still didn't move, Pixie gave an impatient shake of her head. "We are all going together. Get her up, werewolf, and let's go."

Dylan crouched down in front of me and lifted my chin. His almond eyes were soft and concerned, but he also looked confused. His mouth held tension as he seemed to subconsciously absorb my fear. He would probably have never thought twice about going in there.

"Why are you scared?" he asked. "I can smell the fear on your skin, see the dilation in your pupils." He was still holding onto my face, for once not too tightly. My chin nestled in his rough hand like an eggshell splintered with cracks, one wrong move and it would disintegrate. "Do you feel the change in air pressure as it squeezes around you? Or can you smell the weight of the earth as it folds around from all sides?"

I pulled away from the warmth of his palm. "No," I said. "But I probably will now."

He tilted his head and frowned, unable to offer anything further as I looked balefully up at him. There was an awkwardness about him when he tried to interact with me, he wasn't all that good at it, but it was cute, and I appreciated the effort.

"Leave her alone," Chris said. "Or we'll never get her in."

Giving up, I sighed loudly and pushed myself to my feet. Shuffling over the slippery stones, following the only ray of sunlight brave enough to lead the way, I surrendered myself to the rocky prison.

I couldn't appreciate it, but the cave was beautiful. Water so pure and still shone like a mirror over the floor, reflecting the intricately carved ceiling that had been whittled over centuries. Crystals of purple, blue, green, and other indescribable hues peered out of notches. And everywhere I looked, water flowed. It trickled down the walls, pattered from the ceiling and filled my ears with its soothing drone. The air was still warm and humid, but the water was trying its best to cool my blazing skin and with it, drown my panic.

Our footsteps echoed, bouncing off the walls and racing ahead down the narrow passageway. The sun's single ray succumbed and retreated, leaving a dusky grey light. It was barely enough for my strained eyes, but good enough that I could see the rough walls creeping closer. The cave tapered and I reached out both hands to try and keep the walls at bay, my fingers raking over the sharp ridges. The ceiling too had slunk lower, with drops of water persistently showering down as we walked.

Amura came to a halt, and I froze behind her. My

chest rose and fell like I had run a marathon, my heart like a jackhammer against my ribs. I knew what was coming next. At this point, anything was preferable than blindly following her into the squeezing vice.

There was a wide opening at her feet. Water so still not a single ripple interrupted its glassy surface. She slipped into the pool and a grotesque piranha appeared. Its brachycephalic face, the perfect canvas to hold its vicious teeth, grinned widely at me. She turned in the water and dove, red belly flashing. She reappeared a few minutes later, mouth gaping soundlessly and, urgh, it was my turn to follow.

Easing myself slowly into the water, I tried to control my panic. The water was hot, on the verge of being uncomfortable, and there was a dull light emanating from within. I gulped in a large breath and plunged under the water, kicking manically. The red belly of the fish flashed in front, and I swam as fast as I could after it, letting out a small trickle of air as I did.

Following down barely seen twists and turns, the fish eventually flicked its tail upward, and I erupted from the water, gratefully gulping down the moist, dank air. I hauled myself out and onto slippery, warm rocks. There was a small opening in the roof, like a skylight, allowing in a scant, but welcome amount of light. There was no breeze, but I still shivered as I found myself alone.

The minutes ticked by noisily as the silence engulfed me until the pool was again breached. Dylan pulled himself out, water running from his hair and glistening on the auburn stubble lining his chin and cheeks. He eased himself next to me and stared. I looked away as a flush spread through my body, but he raised his hand, gently running his finger down my face.

He cupped my chin and turned my head toward him. His warm breath tickled my skin, stoking the heat between us. This was it. My stomach flipped; my legs tingled.

He leaned in closer. My breath caught as I drank in the sensation, his hand sliding from my face to wind itself around my waist, drawing me tighter against him. The pressure was uncomfortable, his fingers gripping too tightly but his hand was so warm, so strong, so protective.

His heart raced as he pressed hard against my chest. Was he nervous? There was no time to think. He inched closer again, lips parting.

The others are coming.

"Jesus!" I gasped, flinging myself backward and clutching at my heart.

Dylan blinked in surprise, mouth still parted, a slight flush high over his cheekbones.

Chris bobbed up through the watery opening in the cave floor, choking, spluttering and cursing loudly. His hands fumbled at the ledge, unable to grip properly. "Give ... me ... a ... hand?" he panted.

Dylan made no move to help so I went over and hauled him up. He uttered no word of thanks and flopped down, bringing me with him, his body wedged firmly between Dylan and me. Pixie leaped gracefully out next, the droplets running off her body like water off a duck's back. Amura followed, the piranha being momentarily replaced by her human form, red hair standing up in wet spikes, before she changed again into a flying fox, resting upside down from invisible grooves in the ceiling.

As we continued like before, the walls seemed to give me more room to breathe. Even the low ceiling receded as I passed. It was probably in part to the grin that I couldn't keep from my face. It was silly really. I felt like a giddy schoolgirl. I knew that even in the slightest chance we made it out, we would be immediately separated, after the intense testing and interview period was over. Then we would be shipped back off to our respective sides of the fence, forbidden to venture any further into the unknown. Well, unless this experiment was such a roaring success that they tore down all the walls and created the world they preached about. That was more unlikely than walking out of this thing alive.

Sighing, my grin faded and the ceiling drooped back toward me, as if the fatigue of holding up the earth had become too much. At least it had tried.

The soft beat of leathery wings above stopped and Amura reappeared again in human form. We had arrived at a small cavern. There were multiple pools spread out over the floor, their surfaces dark. They may have been an inch deep or endless, the reflective surface giving away no clues. The space was hotter than ever, the air stuffy and muggy.

The only light emanated from a small pixie sitting cross-legged in the center of the cavern. His shimmering hair and placid expression held no disguise. A golden necklace of small bones adorned his throat. In between his crossed legs rested the red backpack.

"Hello, sister." His voice was low and warm, radiating from him like rays of the sun.

I didn't know if he meant the word sister in a platonic sense, but superficial appearance aside, the two of them were like night and day. His face held no deception, and his words had no edge. Just open and honest. I would have done almost anything to have swapped the two of them. As if in reply, the wind guttered around me, sending chill daggers into my body. I crossed my arms tightly, protecting myself as best I could and inched backward to press against the slick wall.

His purple eyes flashed to each of us in turn and

then back to Pixie. "I think you've made the wrong decision."

He chuckled softly but the warmth in his voice was swallowed by the chill wind. The two of them were silent and still. So much unsaid and yet volumes passed between them.

Dylan moved his body like a shield in front of me, blocking my view. My lips pursed as a wave of irritation flew through me. I tried to push him aside, but he was just a solid block of muscle. He looked back at me and raised his thick eyebrows, then resumed his bodyguard position, arms folded, feet firmly planted. Rolling my eyes, I contented myself with shuffling to the side and peering around him.

The wind stopped gusting around us. A moment of inertia fell, as empty as a vacuum.

Pixie's hair swirled around her, first gently and then violently as the gusts picked up force. It lifted her up, invisible fingers clutching and groping, then enveloped her with a rushing swoosh leaving only a shapeless black void hanging in the air.

The peaceful form of the gold pixie sat unconcerned on the floor below whilst the void pulsed above him.

Then the darkness gave a spine-chilling roar and plunged toward him.

NK BROWN

Chapter Fourteen

The golden pixie reacted. He threw out a blinding ray of light directly into the oncoming darkness. The wind shrieked, bunched up as if protecting itself and then swirled around to dive again. The gold pixie's eyes were no longer a serene shade of mauve, they were black and dangerous. The wind tried another assault and lashed into him, tearing and raking with its murderous fingers. Screams of pain were muffled by the roaring laughter of the wind as it circled around again, waiting for another opening to force itself on the unprotected form.

His delicate hand shot out at her, a powerful beam lasered through the heavy air and punched a hole in the rocks by my side. A ray of yellow sunlight snaked its way inside to try and help its comrade. There was a rush of fresh, clean air but with it came a torrent of dust and rocks as the foundations of the cave weakened.

Small crystals pelted down upon me, their jagged edges trying to lodge deeply in my body. My heart pounded in my ears as I flung my arms over my head, a strained mewing noise leaving my tight throat. Every horrendous thought my subconscious mind had ever plied my dreams with erupted into my head and I began to lose my grip on reality.

I was locked inside a coffin, dirt pelting the roof. The clang of a shovel scratching stones as my mother buried me alive.

I was back in the boxcar, being lowered underground. A small hatch opened in the roof and my stepfather's face peered in. He brandished bolt-cutters and with a snap severed the cable. My stomach soared into my mouth as I plunged lower and lower, eternally falling, so deep no one would ever rescue me.

Dylan grabbed my wrists and forced my hands back down to my sides. My chin jutted up as I gasped in air that just wouldn't go any further than my mouth, my lungs screaming for oxygen. As I tried to focus on his face through the blurry tears all I could concentrate on were his hands pinning me hard against the wall. Cutting off any hope of escape as the ceiling continued to crumble down and bury me.

His mouth formed words, but all I could hear was a snarl that blended with the roar of the wind. Chris muscled him violently out of the way and dragged me to the side. His mouth formed the word 'breathe' and the urgency in his brown eyes cut through some of the panic. I wheezed in a scraggly breath and his blurred face nodded. I did it again, feeling the tight belt around my chest loosen a notch.

Another blast of light opened another hole in the wall, directly between me and Dylan. It spewed water like a ruptured fire hydrant, the hot droplets sizzling as they contacted bare flesh. My legs weakened and I sank to the floor.

The cross-legged form of the gold pixie had vanished and now there were two grotesque dark forms, slashing and tearing at each other. One of them was thrown off balance, smashing against the far wall, the other shrieked with pleasure and accelerated toward it.

Another reverberating boom shook the room as one form was impaled against the glittering wall, shards of stone and dust pummeling down from the ceiling. The black shape was stunned and the other sunk its tendrils in deep and dragged it down toward the rippling pool of water on the floor. It was thrust under the glassy surface.

The wind and the light faltered, both desperate to know the outcome.

The flying fox swooped down from the ceiling,

snagged the red backpack and dropped it at my feet. She shot me a look before she swerved away again. We were even. If our competition was over, she would have gifted immunity not only to me, but to the entire human race. My hands shook violently as I pulled it toward me and peeked inside. A faint glint of metal echoed at the bottom. I closed it quickly and pressed it to my back, the click muffled by the running water next to me.

The sunlight retreated out of the splintered hole in the wall and Pixie's shimmering hair reappeared from the inhuman shape. Her arm was outstretched, delicate hand firmly clasped around the swan-like neck of the gold team's pixie. The necklace of golden bones floated serenely on the surface of the water. As she unwound her fingers one by one, the figure slowly disappeared. Sinking into unknown depths, the light was gradually consumed by the pool's dark mouth.

Water still flowed into the cavern beside me, but it had slowed to a trickle. It was now the only sound in the echoing space as it dripped unconcerned onto the wet floor.

"We don't have much time left. We need to keep moving, yes?"

None of us answered.

"Girl, give me the backpack and let's go."

A part of me wondered if once she had the backpack her goal here would be over. Would she kill the rest of us immediately? Only one of us could use the thing at the end anyway. I, like Dylan, wanted nothing to do with the government afterward but immunity for the humans? If they held true to their promise and the Vessel of Unity did indeed exclude humans from the next experiment, then surely the experiment couldn't even run? The whole point was to see if the other beings were ready to interact with us.

"I'll keep it for now," I said.

Pixie's eyes narrowed and I tensed, bracing myself for whichever form of spiteful magic she felt justified the refusal. None came, *this time*.

Turning slowly from me, she stood in front of the small hole in the wall and forced her arms forward. A howling gust of wind broke free and smashed into the crumbling stone. A splintering crack echoed as a large fissure erupted. The soft, mourning rays of the evening sun tentatively reached into the cavern again.

Dylan offered me his hand and this time I took it. He gently pulled me to my feet and steered me toward the opening. I scrambled through, scratching my torn knees further and took a grateful breath of the warm, humid air. The hole was barely wide enough for Dylan's bulky frame to fit through and more crumbling and cracking followed as wide fissures opened behind him. The flying fox soared through quickly and vanished into the tree line.

Once the other two had exited, Pixie led us on a rapid march toward the setting sun and the end of zone five.

Chapter Fifteen

The jungle abruptly ended and stretching out before me was a vast meadow. The fresh breeze was perfumed by the smell of grasses and delicate flowers. It washed over me, cleansing the sweat and stress from my body. I breathed in deeply, filling my lungs, and a smile rose unbidden on my lips.

Glancing over at Dylan, my smile faltered. He was still standing behind the demarcation of the meadow with one hand slowly pulverizing the trunk of an unlucky sapling. His honey eyes were wide. A small trickle of blood crept down his lower lip as his sharp teeth crushed the soft tissue.

Frowning, I turned back to the meadow. There was no danger that I could sense, and the space was a stark relief to the density of the jungle. We had maybe ten minutes of light left. The sky was painted with multiple shades of red, gold, and orange in a beautiful ombre cascading down to the horizon. No clouds littered the pristine space above. There was one large willow tree, a few miles off in the distance. Its heavy branches curled around it, as if pulled by invisible hands, protecting its heart center.

The instructions are in. They are a little basic.

I turned to the others who had all stepped onto the soft, rustling grass of the meadow, except for Dylan. He seemed trapped by the forest, an invisible barrier preventing him from leaving.

"Zone four," I said, "pass through the meadow."

"That's it?" Chris asked.

I nodded.

Pixie was gazing off into the distance. Her long hair shimmered in the slight breeze as she swayed slightly, at one with all the elements around her.

"I can see the demarcation for the next zone." Her voice floated around me, as if coming from the air itself. "It's directly across from here, not far, even for human legs. You can see it too, werewolf, yes?"

Dylan made no reply.

"Then let's get as far as we can, whilst we still have light left," Chris said.

"We cannot just run blindly through the field, human," Amura chided. "We do not know if any of the other teams have progressed this far. Even without the Vessel of Unity, if the teams are intact, they still pose a danger."

"Come on, Anna, *we* are the only ones in danger here," Chris said, ignoring Amura and turning to me. "Leave them and let's go."

He glanced at my backpack. Did he genuinely think we would be better to stick together, or did he only want to stay within snatching distance of the Vessel of Unity? If I were to die, he could probably still save himself.

Without waiting for any further discussion, he snuck another glance at the backpack and then strode off through the grass, leaving a trail of crushed stems and broken flowers behind him. Pixie leapt after him, feet so light not a mark was left behind. The breeze sighed heavily, inviting me to follow.

I turned back to Dylan. "Are you ready?"

His eyes snapped to my face. I couldn't read the expression behind them. Fear? Guilt? He blew out a hot breath, causing the skin on my face to tingle, as if singed. He moved reluctantly over the line of demarcation, the last rays of the sun causing his auburn hair to burn like fire.

"You should go on ahead with them," he said.

"No, we're supposed to be a team."

He looked unconvinced. He stopped again, and his nostrils flared, sensing something I had no knowledge of.

"How are you going to protect me from way over here anyway?" I meant it as a joke. The look he gave me wiped the half smile from my lips. There was no reason for it, but my heart squeezed painfully in my chest. Sweat beaded on my skin and scuttled down my back.

He gave a subtle twitch of his hand, gesturing for me to move forward. We walked together, not touching, not talking. Amura leapt into the air and the streamlined body of a cardinal shot up and into the twilight, the tufts on its head standing up like daggers against the sky.

Eventually I broke the silence. "I don't think Pixie likes us very much. Why do you think she is so attached to Chris?"

Uninvited, the wind circled back with a reply. "Because, girl. You are not here for the sake of the unity. You have your own agenda, no? Whereas the rest of us know how important this is. How many lives will be changed for the better because of the outcome. It would be easier for me to tolerate you, if you stopped thinking about yourself and started thinking about the world as a whole, yes?"

I groaned quietly and grimaced at Dylan, expecting some form of comradery. But his face remained unchanged, his thoughts elsewhere. There was no way Pixie's motive for wanting the unity was pure. She had been the one quite happy to destroy any other being that came across her path.

I tried again to make conversation. "Do you have another random question to ask me, Dylan?"

"I hope you forgive easily," he whispered. His eyes were trained on the floor and there was a slump to his shoulders and a drag in his step.

"Wait!" In front of us, Pixie held up her hand.

Out of the twilight another being emerged. Her elegant figure materialized from the shadows, rising from the ground as if created from a single breath of Mother Nature herself. Her hair barely tickled her ears, but it still emitted the same captivating shimmer, dazzling and sparkling like diamonds. Coiled around her neck was a segmental brown necklace. The pieces formed from a jumble of insect anatomy—beetle shells, worm tails, centipede plates.

Sliding between her feet, noiselessly winding through the long grass, was a brown anaconda. Its forked tongue lazily tasted the air. There was a satiated sluggishness to its movement as it dragged its distended abdomen.

"Where is the rest of your team? You should all be together, no?" Pixie asked.

"They are safe." The brown team pixie spoke in a warm, earthly voice. The snake remained passive at her feet. "We have come to guide you through zone four. There are many perils laid out before you and we can see you safely to the Chasm. Our instructions say we cannot enter alone and must do so alongside another team. We thought it wise to leave our weaker members under the protection of our wolf whilst we sought out others."

Pixie returned the polite explanation with a deadly calm stare. The wind fled toward her. With a flick of her little finger, it sidled like tendrils of mist toward the visitors. The brown pixie offered no resistance. The snake bunched around her feet, its scales overlapping like an accordion as the wind probed.

"You see, we have nothing to hide," the brown pixie said.

The wind flapped in annoyance, circling back

around to draw us closer together.

"I cannot read her," Pixie hissed. "And the snake is blocking me as well. They are not to be trusted. You agree, wolf, yes?"

Dylan was paying no attention. His face was neutral, his thoughts drawn inwards, consumed by a private conversation.

"We're not going to kill them, Pixie," I said. An invisible force seemed to be pulling me toward the strangers, whispering for me to trust them. It echoed through my bones. "Let's work together and get through this zone. We stand more chance of being successful if we use their knowledge. And besides, we outnumber them, if that thought makes you braver."

Taunting Pixie gave me such a childish pleasure that it took all my strength not to burst into laughter.

"I'm not scared of them, you idiot girl."

"You're not? Well, in that case, maybe we can let them lead us, no?" I failed at stopping the grin from breaking onto my face.

"That is such a wise decision," the brown pixie's voice cut through the gusts of wind. "Anna, honey, come and walk with me in front. I have many things to share with you."

My grin melted. There had only ever been one person that called me 'honey'. A tremor of hope, a belief in the impossible seeped into my bloodstream.

Anna. Don't...

The spirit's voice was muted. Their words interrupted by static. I pushed on, leaving the others to follow in my wake. Even Dylan lagged, but he still seemed to be aware of where I was. Every time his amber eyes shifted from the ground to my back a ripple of warmth flowed through me.

"It seems you already know the fate of the gold

and blue teams," the brown pixie said.

There was a slight fog in her eyes, the creeping shadow of twilight covering the purple irises. The snake's vapid black eyes held the same. It was subtle, though, and with the deepening night it may have just been my exhausted mind imagining it.

"We met with the green team early in zone five," she continued. "They had been given a poltergeist as their supernatural ally. You remember the bedtime stories read to you as a child, Anna, honey?"

I did remember. My heart thumped painfully against my ribs. But how did she know?

"Well, as I'm sure you recall, they are the most distrustful of the spirit world. Some are merely impish, spending their eternity pranking and jesting the living, but in every barrel, there are always rotten apples. The green team couldn't tell just by looking that theirs was bad. On the outside it appeared perfect, shiny and whole. But as they bit deeper, the core was black. Turned into a gelatinous mash of decay.

"We stumbled upon them and discovered that this particular poltergeist had possessed one of their weaker humans. It then replicated, spreading like mold through the rest of the team. Manipulating their brains to express their most base urges, reverting them to their primitive selves. They self-destructed very quickly. Of course, the poltergeist was destroyed as well, having killed its hosts."

"Why would the government have put it on a team?"

She uttered a single laugh. "Have you not realized the staggering level of bias that occurs during the experiment? I suppose the propaganda you humans are spoon-fed blame every other species but your own. Really, Anna. Did you not learn anything from my life teachings?"

The candle of hope sputtered again. Could I ask? How did this pixie know these things about my life? But if it wasn't true, then how would I go on?

"The green team were supposed to control the poltergeist, to harness it. If they worked together, they could use it on their enemies. But alas, they did not."

The flame ignited. It was time. I had to ask. Had to know. Sucking in a deep breath I whispered, "Who is the spirit on your team?"

"It's me, honey. Your father."

NK BROWN

Chapter Sixteen

The flame of hope erupted. This was it. Here he was. Now I could learn the truth about what had happened. I spun around to grin at Dylan, but he and the others had fallen behind. Just three silhouettes bunched together with a small bird form on one of their shoulders. They were moving slowly, as if their feet were stuck in molasses or clotted mud. The earth below my feet was fresh and dry. Hardly an indentation from my path through the meadow showed in the dark behind.

It hit me suddenly that there was no breeze.

"What is it, honey?" the brown pixie asked.

"We should wait for the others to catch up."

The snake hissed softly and butted against my knees, forcing me forward.

"We have many important things to discuss first, I think. A little privacy would be a marvelous idea, don't you think, Anna, honey?"

I turned again. Dylan's amber eyes shone in the gloom, glued to my face. The snake shoved me forward again and I stumbled a few paces further.

"Come on, Anna, you must have so many questions to ask me. Here's your chance." The pixie was no longer smiling. The mist in her eyes thickened as she leaned toward me. "How did I die? Why didn't I come and find you? Did I know you possessed the traits of a medium?"

She gripped my arm. Her hand was gritty, nails black with dirt. I tried to turn again but she held firm, forcing me to maintain eye contact.

"If you let me in Anna, honey, I can tell you everything."

A pawing sensation prickled my skin like a cat

needling for leverage on a pillow.

"I don't know what you mean and I'm waiting for—"

"Open your mind, honey. Like I taught you. You remember our experiments? I can possess you and then you'll never lose me again."

The prickling intensified, as if a hookworm was trying to burrow through my skin. Forcing its way through my pores so it could attach.

I wrenched out of her grasp and tripped over the snake, landing heavily on my ass. I started to scramble backward but the snake reared, fangs elongating with the shadows of the night. It leered at me, trapping me at the pixie's feet.

"Oh, Anna, honey, what a shame. We'll have to do it the hard way I suppose." The brown pixie stamped her foot and the ground shook beneath us. Large fissures raced across the meadow ripping the grass and flowers out from their roots. "Hurry, her team is almost here. This won't stop them for long."

The snake's nostrils flared before it plunged toward my throat. I grabbed for the annihilator and missed, twisting my body so that the snake's fangs glanced down my arm. My gut churned as the scent of strawberry shampoo wafted up from the depths of its stomach and belched over me.

I jabbed my foot into its neck, hoping to stun it, but the thick muscle barely twitched.

It rose again before me. My fingers fumbled for the handle of the annihilator. Before I could reach it, the snake lunged. My fist closed around the fabric of the backpack, and I ripped it from my back and held it in front of my face. The snake's powerful jaws clamped down, its fangs sinking into the soft material. It jerked back with a spasm of pain as it connected with the canteen. I threw myself to the side and scrambled to my feet, colliding with a wall of solid muscle.

Another tremor shook the ground, spinning the air around me. Dylan's arm ratcheted me to him, pinning me against his chest as he spread his weight and rode the quake. The wind was blustering again, causing chunks of dirt and beheaded flowers to tornado through the air.

Peeking out from under Dylan's arm, both the brown team pixie and the snake had vanished.

I braced myself for Pixie's upcoming tirade. Would it be worse than getting impaled by a ten-foot snake?

"Idiot girl!"

No hint of mist lightened the furious black pits of her eyes. On the plus side, at least she wasn't possessed, so that was something.

"No, I am not possessed, but once again your ignorance almost destroyed this team, no? If that poltergeist had taken you, which would be no personal loss to me, it would have ended our competition! You would have single-handedly destroyed the union once again, yes?"

Calm her down, Anna. We need to keep moving. They are still out there watching, waiting for another opportunity to attack.

"Where were you? A little heads up would've been nice. Maybe something like, 'oh, hey, Anna. That's not really your father's spirit. It's a sociopathic poltergeist trying to possess you'."

You tuned me out. I understand, Anna. Hope is an addictive game. We keep rolling that dice, even when the odds are not in our favor because there is always a chance. It's what makes us human. It keeps us alive.

"Stop talking to voices in your head!" Chris cut in. "I've already warned you once."

Dylan growled a warning, the sound rumbling deep within his chest. He resumed scanning the meadow, but his thoughts drifted, eyes slightly glazed. A solitary bead of sweat crawled down his face.

"Look, guys," I said, "I'm sorry, okay? We're halfway through this meadow now so if we stick together, we can finish. That's the whole point of this ridiculous thing, right?"

"I think you need to remind yourself of that the most, girl, no? Stop harboring that asinine idea of reuniting with your dead father and we'll *all* get out of this alive, yes?"

Dylan's answering growl was lost over another rumbling earthquake. Amura launched from Dylan's shoulder as the red cardinal and piped a warning, zooming off in the direction of the demarcation at the end of the meadow. Chris shoved me forward, side-stepping around Dylan who snarled at him. Pixie leapt over a deep trench that had split in the ground at our feet and united with Chris, the two of them marching onward without checking for me and Dylan.

The ground lay silent again as we walked, but a new sound filtered through the darkness.

Chapter Seventeen

The howl was unnatural. It held the melancholy, rumbling notes of a wolf but was laced with a chilling, metallic ringing. A pulse of fear sunk deep into my abdomen, impinging on my nerves and weakening my legs.

Pixie and Chris increased their pace. They seemed to be moving unnaturally fast, as if the wind was scooping up each footfall and forcing them forward. Soon they were almost invisible, swallowed by the black hole of night.

We approached the huge boughs of the willow and Dylan froze. The coarse hairs on his arm stood up straight, his back slightly bowed as if his hackles were raised. He ground his teeth, the stubble on his jaw slowly moving back and forth in an unsettling rhythm. His hands started to curl up by his sides and once again his whole being was focused on something up ahead that I was unable to see.

A frantic whistle came from inside the tree and the cardinal fixed its beady eye on me, head cocked to the side. Behind, the luminescent glow of the moon started to appear. It slithered into the black sky, a perfectly round, brilliant stain on the inky black night. I grabbed Dylan's arm and dragged him toward the tree. His feet barely moved, and my breath strained loud and panicked with the exertion in the quiet air. Once he was fully enveloped in the tree's shadow, I let him go.

His voice was louder than usual, anger having seeped into it, metamorphosizing his usual calming tone. "You need to run. Leave me and go. When I change, I will kill you."

"You don't need to change, Dylan. Stay human.

Remember who you are. Focus on something else, something that means a lot to you, your life, your family, anything." My voice was barely a whisper. "I'll be right here."

He didn't look at me, didn't respond. Every muscle in his body tensed, primed as if ready to explode. I did the only thing I could think of. The only thing I knew how to do. Tentatively, I curled my arm around his and took his hand in mine, lacing our fingers together. I stood still, barely breathing, focusing on calming my raging heart. His hand quivered in mine, grip so tight that spears of pain shot up my arm.

Time ticked slowly on, second by second as Dylan fought for control of his body. Fought against nature. Fought the overwhelming urge to kill me.

The howl rang into the still air again. Closer than before.

"Dylan?" My voice was barely audible. He didn't reply, remaining staring out into the distance. "How did you end up here?"

I had millions of questions I wanted to ask him, but I chose something he may actually answer. He still didn't look at me, but after a long silence he let out a small sigh of defeat.

"It used to be just a sport," he said. "My dad showed us how to do it and not get caught. But my brother wanted more excitement, he wanted to go further. To venture far beyond the fence." Random words shot out loudly between the whispers as he talked, far too noisy and uncontrolled in the quiet night. "Sometimes we missed our target, or they had weapons, but mostly it was easy. It even began to become boring, like we were just doing chores."

I remained quiet, listening intently to the jumbled sentences. The moon continued to slink across the sky toward us.

"But in the beginning..." he paused as he took a deep breath, a smile creeping onto his face as his lips parted, exposing the points of his teeth, "it was such a rush. The thrill of the chase made me feel alive. I could sense the fear, smell the sweat from miles away. Every terrified breath would reverberate through the air and flood my body with adrenaline." His voice had risen again, the growl of excitement rumbling deep within him.

The silvery shadow of the moon reached the edge of the willow. It was trying to penetrate the thick cage of her arms, but she held firm.

"Before I met you, I didn't realize there was any other way."

I had forgotten about the experiment. Forgotten about the timeline. His hand locked in mine and the haunting words floating in my mind consumed me. A light breeze rustled through the grass. The woody stems swayed in place, displaced momentarily as if something was slithering through them.

"There were always stories floating around about how we all once lived peacefully together. But there was still so much hate. Too many violent memories burning strongly, especially in those of us that patrolled the fence. My grandfather's parents were taken as volunteers before the experiment was devised. They were made to live in a small commune surrounded by humans. Forced into servitude, locked up every full moon. The eyes of the world upon them, daring them to resist. Hoping they would get the chance to witness the vulgar truth as they exposed their dark side. Their primal urges."

A dark, wispy cloud crawled across the sky, its passage hampered by unseen forces that were holding it back.

"There was a massacre. The ugly truth *was*

revealed. But it wasn't from the werewolves. My grandfather managed to escape, but he was the only one. He does not count himself as lucky. He still bears the scars, the stain permanently etched on his soul as the memories smolder within."

I shifted uncomfortably. His nails dug deeper into my flesh in response to the movement. The dark cloud edged closer to the glowing moon. For the first time I started to feel a beginning of hope. The chance of escape was coming.

"Why did *you* volunteer to come here?" he asked.

The flicker of hope sputtered as a weight pressed heavily upon my chest. I didn't want to talk about it. I didn't want to remember. I turned slowly to Dylan. A muscle pulsed in his cheek, the veins in his neck standing out against the strained olive skin. I tried to draw in a deep breath, but the air stuck in my throat. "Humans don't volunteer, Dylan."

I thought about the small kitchen. About the whirring ceiling fan. About the four other bodies pressed elbow to elbow around the notched table. It made sense that Becky would go against the plan. Ever since I had known her, she had liked to be different. To rebel in her own way. She openly resented coming to live with us in the cramped house. Had preferred her life when it was just her and her father. Why would she vote for him, the only constant presence she had ever known when she had a guilt-free option sitting next to her?

The plan had been for my stepfather to vote for my mother, but he too must have decided on his own route. Maybe he thought that there was no harm in throwing in my name when the odds were stacked against him anyway. But even so, two votes out of five was not enough for me to win.

Another breeze sidled through the grass,

encircling the willow. A low hiss emitted from its path.

"We need to run." My voice was barely audible, less than a whisper. "Once the cloud covers the light. Run for the end."

A snarl escaped his lips, and a shiver ran unbidden up my spine. In the tree above, the cardinal shifted, softly spreading out her feathers ready to fly. Dylan forced his head around with a crack and his eyes locked onto mine. There was pain on his face and anguish. But above all, hatred. Not of me, but of himself.

He dug his nails deeper into the bruised flesh of my hand. I gritted my teeth and held my breath to stop the whimper escaping from my dry lips.

A piercing whistle cut through the tension. The loud flap of wings and rustle of branches screamed down from above and Dylan pulled me forward out of the willow's embrace and into the night. I ran after him, legs flying. He was so much faster that he dragged me, my feet incapable of keeping pace.

My lungs burned in my chest, unable to get enough oxygen. My heart had never recovered from the constant panic of the last day and was weakly vibrating, on the verge of giving up. The edges of my vision dimmed, and the grass swayed in front of me rippling like a lake. Somehow, I kept moving. Dylan's strong grip forced me not to fall behind.

The cloud covered the moon, but it was determined to keep moving along in its journey across the sky. Small shards of silvery light peeked out of the other side. I forced my legs to move faster still. The grass was a blur below me, tugging at my legs as I ran, trying to slow me down. In the distance the meadow ended. There was nothing but a blank emptiness behind.

Pixie and Chris were huddled at the demarcation. Her hair shimmered in the dark, seeming to give off its own light, like a beacon. But as my eyes focused on her it became clear. She wasn't giving off her own light.

She was reflecting the moonlight.

Dylan's hand let go of mine as a snarl ripped through his body. He pushed me roughly away and my feet caught immediately. I smacked into the ground with so much force I slid through the grass, the woody stems lacerating my palms.

Fur sprouted over his body, racing up his strained muscles. His teeth elongated and cracked together as his jaw lengthened, lips peeling grotesquely away. A heavy thump shook my body as his hands landed on the ground, barely feet from my face. Long claws extended with the metallic ring of a switchblade.

Amura gave another shrill whistle of warning, and the tiny cardinal plummeted down from the sky. Its razor-sharp beak raked across the eyes of the werewolf, causing a howl of pain and frustration to boom through the night.

Slamming my raw hands against the earth, I pushed off, my feet scrambling for purchase. I raced toward the black end of the meadow, not caring what lay on the other side.

The pounding of four large feet closed in, the familiar scent of cinnamon and spices drowning me. As I leapt forward into the inky blackness, his claws grabbed my shoulders, digging into the sweat-soaked skin. Sharp, wet teeth closed around the back of my neck.

The weight of his hot body pressed into mine as we both fell, locked together, down into the unknown.

Chapter Eighteen

We fell, locked together for what seemed like an eternity. Blackness pressed all around, not a shard of light to be seen. The wind rushed past my ears and tangled in my hair. Falling in the dark was a lot less frightening than falling in the light. Not being able to see the floor rushing toward me meant my brain could not prepare for the impact. It couldn't warn itself that death was approaching. Dylan's hot body encircled my back, nails tearing into my shoulders, mouth pressed hard against the bare skin of my neck.

The wind gusting past slowed, the howling becoming a gentle whisper and very lightly my feet touched solid ground. Dylan landed behind me, and he slowly retracted each of his claws. My skin tugged and stung as cold sweat oozed into each gash.

"I'm so sorry." His voice whispered directly into my ear, full of guilt.

I didn't reply. My shoulders screamed in pain and my whole body ached from the exertion of running from him. He still had his hands on me, lightly now, and the warmth I found so comforting before did nothing to stop the shivers creeping up my body. The stubble on his face softly grazed my neck as he sighed and stepped away.

For the first time in almost a day, I missed the life I had left. The routine, the comfort, the safety. I bit my lip, unable to stop the tears from streaming down my face, glad no one could see in the dark.

A pair of heavy feet landed with a thump next to me, the fading smell of cigarettes swirling around in the pitch-black emptiness. A whirring and a soft click followed as a small flame flickered. Chris's face was distorted, the shadows crawled over his skin, the corners of his mouth appearing to droop down to his jaw like a wooden puppet.

A tickling sensation crept up my bare arm like someone had a feather and was barely touching my flesh. The chill ascended my body as the fine hairs on the back of my neck stood up. In the dim light of the flame, was a large hairy tarantula. Red knees rhythmically pumping as its sharp feet tiptoed up my skin.

I watched, fascinated as it reached my shoulder and halted. The light reflected back at me in its multiple beady eyes. I felt strangely comforted that she had chosen to be with me. This fleeting feeling of pleasure was rapidly replaced by revulsion as the tiny fangs scraped the new blood out of the claw marks and into her gaping mouth.

You should all rest whilst you can.

"Where have you been?" I spoke quietly but my voice reverberated around, eerily distorted.

Someone else needed me more. Have the others stay close and I will guard us.

A cold red flame materialized in front of me, the shape oddly human. I repeated the spirit's words to the others and looked around in the dark. There was no light other than the small one Chris had. Chris gratefully collapsed onto the floor, but I hesitated.

Turning around, Dylan was watching me intently. His arms were tightly crossed over his chest, fingers gripping the sleeves of his shirt, knuckles white. I knew he wanted my forgiveness. He wanted to be close to me. My stomach twisted and I sucked in a deep breath, turning away from him and settling down alone.

Wrapping my cold arms around myself, the empty feeling grew. From atop my shoulder the tarantula gave an irritated shake of her head. I ignored her and she went back to cleaning up the wounds.

The temperature was slowly falling, my breath misting in front of my eyes, swirling up and around to join whatever lay in the shadows. And there were definitely beings in the shadows. I couldn't see them, but I knew they were there. I could sense their curiosity, sense their excitement and sense their suspicion coming from all around. It was the spine-chilling sense of being watched when you knew you were alone. And even surrounded by my teammates, I was alone.

Part of me wanted to reach back and grab Dylan's hand. But instead, I dug my freezing hands into my pockets. As I did, my fingers touched something—the soft, velvety petals of the poppy. It was remarkably intact from everything it had suffered that day, and I closed my fist around it, pulling it out and pressing it against my nose. The memory of the open field full of the beautiful scent of spring came racing back to my mind and I clung to it.

The cold pressed in, its breath unrelenting and my shivers increased. As the sound of my chattering teeth clashing together echoed around the cavern, Dylan came over. He wrapped his warm arms tightly around me and the heat from his body began to thaw my resistance. As I didn't pull away, he stayed there, and I drew my knees up into my chest and let him hold me.

"That's why you always smell of flowers," he whispered, as his breath warmed the space between us.

I was glad that was the odor I was giving off.

"Why do you smell of cinnamon?" I asked.

He let out a soft snort. "No idea."

Leaning my head against his chest, I listened to the gentle thudding of his heart. Angling my face upward I was able only to see his outline in the dark. His breath fell warmly upon my skin, kissing against my lips in the dark with every shallow exhale. But he held the distance between us, even though he could have closed it instantly. Maybe out of respect? Maybe from uncertainty as to how I would react. But he was trying again. The thought warmed me.

"Tell me something about you," he whispered.

"Do you want to be more specific?"

He blew a snort of laughter into my hair. "Okay, then. How about you tell me about a recurring dream you have. Something weird or unexplainable and I'll tell you what it means."

"Why? Dreams aren't real. They're just a jumble of subconscious thoughts."

"Some are, but there are lots that can be understood from a recurring one. Something that you know you've had many times over, even if you forget it instantly on waking." His arms tightened around me, and my cold muscles began to heat. "The head of the Demi-Government, a centaur, she made it compulsory that astrology and oneirology were taught in all schools. My dad dragged me out of school last year, so I've forgotten some of it."

"Why did he want you to leave school?"

"It becomes optional at eighteen and he wanted me to patrol the fence, like him." His arms ratcheted tighter, the pressure like a belt a notch too tight. My ribcage fought to expand, my body pulling away. He realized what he was doing and relaxed again. "Sorry," he whispered. "So, tell me."

"My father used to do lots of weird experiments. Most of the time it would be in the basement. I was never allowed down there, for he kept it locked, even from my mother. Sometimes I would see a sliver of the room as he left. It was chaotic, boxes overflowing, shelves sagging under the weight of instruments and papers and maps. But occasionally he would bring up an object for me to study."

Our voices were hushed, the sound barely carrying in the gloom, but Amura was listening intently, having stopped gorging herself on my shoulder. Pixie and Chris had their backs to us, both breathing in the soporific pattern of sleep, but a prickle crept up my spine as I imagined Pixie's mauve irises open and vacant as she turned her attention to us. Storing any information that may come in useful for whatever scheme she was hatching.

"He had relics from before the separation, pieces from all the species," I continued. "He said that if you opened your mind and focused, then the memory stored in the object would transfer to you. You could see its owner, its use, its journey in life. He said some would hear words and others would see pictures, you just had to empty your mind to be the vessel it needed for communication. For all objects wanted to share their story."

I kept focused on the outline of Pixie. She lay on her side, breath still rhythmic, but her hair trickled away from her ear, pooling on the floor as if a whisper of wind had caressed her face.

"Anyway, I wanted it to be true and I did what he said. I heard nothing and saw nothing. But I began to have a recurring dream. It was difficult to make sense of, but whenever I fell into that world, my subconscious knew it was the same one that I experienced before, and if I accepted the flow and went where my thoughts guided, then every time I would go further.

"Different voices would narrate passages in my head. Fairytales, essays, speeches. There would be so many—some shouting, some whispering, some nonsensical. When I would wake up, covered in sweat and tangled in my sheets, my father would be right there staring at me. A notepad in his hand, pen poised a millimeter from the page, ready to carve the fantasy of a dream into reality.

"As always, I knew I had disappointed him. He wrote down everything I said, locked the notepad away with his research, told me how interesting it was, but there was something missing. He never said it, but there was expectation in his wide eyes and tilted body that would fizzle as I spoke. Once he told me I needed to compartmentalize. To focus only on one voice and everything would become clearer. My mother put a stop to these experiments once she found out and we never spoke of them after that."

"What happened to his stuff after he died? Did you go down there and find anything?"

"No." I shrugged. "My mother got rid of it all. The night he left for the experiment. I was distracted, ear pressed against the radio waiting for an announcement or any update. I didn't know anything had happened until I dragged myself into the kitchen the next morning, still clutching the radio and passed by the door to the basement. It was swinging from the hinges, lock broken, an incandescent bulb illuminating the naked room. Not a shred of evidence left behind, every memory erased."

"I'm really sorry, Anna."

I shrugged again.

"You know, I dreamt of you before I'd even met you." His voice was barely a breath upon my face, his finger gently tracing circles on my arm. "I didn't see you clearly, but I could smell you, sense you and when I saw you in the clearing it was like everything had clicked into place."

I swallowed, not sure I'd forgotten the feel of his claws raking through my muscles, his teeth spearing into my neck. He was trying to apologize, but even if he felt like that now, what was stopping him from shifting again and killing me?

He kissed my hair softly, gently pulling my head back toward him. I was too exhausted to resist and melted into his chest. The smell of the fresh poppy hung between us, mixing with his cinnamon spice as I pressed into him.

The rhythmic clicking of Amura's pincers began again, blending with the dull thuds of Dylan's heart, dragging my eyelids shut and escorting me toward sleep.

NK BROWN

Chapter Nineteen

"Any instructions yet?" Chris's voice echoed in the dark space. The lighter clicked as his fingers numbly cranked at the small dial.

I sat up stiffly. Any part of my body that was not protected by the warmth of Dylan's strong form was painfully cold. Prickles like the pointed tips of needles stabbed any exposed skin and the shivers resumed their assault on my body as my conscious mind began to stir. The tarantula was still perched on my shoulder, its spiny black hairs writhing along its legs as if they were a field of snakes in the flickering light.

Welcome to zone three. The chasm between the living and the dead. Your task is to set someone free.

The red form of the spirit hovered in the center of our small group, spilling a faint glow onto our faces like we were sitting around a campfire. But no warmth reached out with the red fingers of flame.

"So, what else is down here?" Dylan whispered.

There was a rustle of fabric as someone shifted position. Surprisingly, both Pixie and Chris were quiet.

"The Chasm is filled with the souls of those beings that couldn't decide which way to go," I said.

That is a very simplified way of putting it.

"That's the explanation you gave me!"

Yes, well. A simple explanation for a simple mind.

"Hilarious," I muttered.

More specifically, the Chasm is filled with those souls that still had some unfinished business. The indecision about whether to let go and progress onto the afterlife or to remain and try to fulfil their destiny led them to this purgatory.

I repeated the spirit's more succinct explanation

to Dylan.

"Don't be fooled into thinking that we are surrounded by angelic beings that have some higher purpose to fulfil. There will be more wronged souls out for revenge than noble ideals down here," Chris said.

There will always be ideas and morals you do not agree with or understand, but that does not make them wrong.

"I know that the government locked them down here for a reason. To stop the espionage that was tearing everyone apart."

That is not why the portal was closed. Nor was it why the Unified Government shattered.

A silence fell. Chris's heavy breathing was the only sound in the darkness. His face was lit by grotesque shadows in the small flame from his lighter. As his voice had swelled in the darkness, Dylan moved closer to me again. His arm lightly touched mine, the coarse hairs scratching against my skin. Amura had not moved from her perch on my shoulder, as still as death itself.

Pixie's silky voice lightly gusted through the silence. "It is my understanding, that this was the original experiment, no? A way in which to see how different beings interacted with each other in a world with nothing to lose. If the government closed the portal, then no word could drift back to the living and no warning fly ahead to the dead. The perfect petri dish in which to watch history repeat itself, again and again."

I listened to all their words and thought the truth probably lay somewhere in the middle. There was no way my father would have passed straight onto the afterlife. He was always so outspoken in his views about unifying everyone again. He definitely would have unfinished business. I had to find him and then I would persuade the others to release him. Dylan would side with me, and

Amura would probably choose me over the other two as well. But what would the spirit's choice be?

Irritatingly, pixie had read my mind or at least sensed it. Her mouth twitched into a smirk, her eyes narrowed, looking inky black in the gloom. "Don't get any ideas, girl. We stay together down here, or they will consume you like any other naïve do-gooders that make the mistake of falling in."

I tried to push thoughts of my father far from my mind and out of her reach.

Pixie flashed her eyes at Dylan. "Keep close to her, wolf. Should be easy for you, no? We don't want the thrill of the chase to overcome your feeble resolve. Again."

Dylan's snarl crackled in the thin air. He launched himself at Pixie, knocking me sideways with the force of a cannon. Chris scurried out of the dim circle of red light and was engulfed by the darkness.

Pixie moved not a muscle.

Dylan slammed into an invisible wall, nails slicing with a metallic ring.

I leapt toward Dylan, wrapping both my arms around one of his. The backpack lifted from my back as if snagged on an invisible hook. Letting go of his arm I whirled around. Nothing living stirred behind me. Amura clicked her spider's beak and pointed with one of her hairy legs. The zipper was half open, the canteens and food exposed.

"What is it?" Dylan tore his gaze from Pixie and whipped his head around, nose twitching.

"Nothing," I said. "I think I must have imagined it."

I yanked the zipper closed. Had I imagined it? I probably hadn't closed it properly and the sudden movement caused it to open further. The feeling of unease died as quickly as it came, the tendrils of fog from a forgotten dream dissolving into the ether upon waking.

"Seriously, what?" Dylan lowered his face into mine, hands clawing my shoulders.

Amura scurried over to him and sank her beak into the webbing between his thumb and finger. Dylan snarled but released me.

"I thought something was trying to get the Vessel of Unity from my pack," I said.

He turned back toward Pixie, his muscles coiling underneath him as he prepared to spring again.

"It wasn't me, wolf. There are numerous other beings down here. Even the dead can steal. If I wanted it, I could take it. She's just a human. They are weak. Their only strength lies in their numbers, no?"

His weight rocked back to his heels as he scrutinized her, but the tension remained in his erect posture.

"Dylan, I really may have imagined it." I pulled him away from Pixie again. "We should get going. The longer we stay down here the worse it's going to get. The stillness is creepy, and it is messing with my mind."

"Yes, your human *handler* is correct, wolf. You really must keep some control over that temper of yours, no?"

I gaped at her. Even Amura turned all her glassy eyes in her direction.

A lanky shadowed outline expanded behind the invisible wall. The shape solidified above Pixie.

It was not a spirit.

Chapter Twenty

Chris stepped out of the dark, his small lighter distorting his shadowed self as he joined Pixie. "Have you finished bickering?" When no one replied he said, "Let's go then."

Reluctantly we set off into the dark, the flickering red flame of the spirit guiding the way. The Chasm seemed to stretch on for an eternity. The air was damp and stale and with every breath I felt unrefreshed, like the one I had just taken was empty. Our footsteps rang out loudly, announcing our progress to every abandoned soul down there. I kept my thoughts as far away from finding my father as I could—and therefore away from Pixie—focusing instead on Dylan's demeaner as he stalked beside me.

His muscles were starting to relax, his arms lengthening by his sides. With every footfall a burst of heat would soar through me as his hand grazed mine. It was interesting that Dylan's first suspicion had been Pixie tampering with my backpack as well. It could have been another being down here or just simply a trick of my mind. If we could escape Pixie for a few moments, I would find out what he thought.

The two of them shared a mutual animosity from day one. They couldn't possibly know each other but there was some kind of history there. The Magic Government had always been the closest to the humans. They were responsible for strengthening the fence and the forests, the only protection that the humans had from the others. Maybe that was why he didn't trust her?

As we continued, colors started to emerge. Flashes and glimpses of green, blue and gold appeared in the shadows. A low humming vibrated through the dark, prickling my skin as it washed over me. The further we walked, the stronger and more numerous the apparitions became. They stopped skulking at the edges of my vision and started to take forms. All guttering like candle flames, pressing in from the sides. The mirage of fire but bringing nothing but chills.

"Are we going to find your daughter down here?" I whispered.

I am going to make sure she is finally at peace.

Now I was conflicted. I wanted to help find their daughter. To reunite them. But I also had to know. Had to know if my father was down here. And, if I found him would I be able to *not* save him? Releasing him as a spirit, or whichever form he took, which way would he go? And in which plane would I see him again?

As usual, Chris's voice cut through my thoughts with his own opinion. "We should save someone who is going to make a difference. Someone who can help bring about the unity. That is the whole point of this experiment after all."

His words were right, but I had the strange sense that his motivations were not so pure. In the dark, Pixie's hair shimmered as she turned to him.

"I agree, Chris. There are many powerful beings down here that would be able to work their influence. Many were persecuted because of their alliance with the magic folk, and these would be a good find, no?"

Dylan murmured something in my ear, quiet enough so that even the wind couldn't carry the words away.

The discussion between Pixie and Chris continued. It veered the closest they had come yet to a disagreement. Chris was adamant they needed a human and Pixie wanted any other kind of being, even though they both professed to want the same outcome. The echo of our footsteps bounced back quicker than before, reverberating off invisible walls. We entered a narrow passageway and in the flickering light a dim fork emerged up ahead. Both options were dark and airless and neither inviting.

The red flame of the spirit turned right, Pixie's shimmering hair followed, and the sound of a quietly controlled argument drifted away. Dylan grabbed my arm in the dark and swung me left.

It was pitch-black without the red flame and my eyes widened, hopelessly trying to squeeze any shapes into my mind, but I remained blind. Even though the way was smooth, I stumbled along. The arm not trapped in Dylan's strong grip groping the empty space in front of me.

"Where are we going?" I hissed at him. "Can you even see anything?"

"My eyes are better than yours," came the whispered reply. "I want to make it up to you."

We began sloping downhill, just gradually at first but soon I noticed the pull on my legs with every step. I dug in my heels, forcing Dylan to stop.

"We need to find the others, this is ridic—"

"Keep your voice down," he growled, mouth very close to my ear.

I had a momentary image of his sharp white teeth puncturing the back of my neck, dagger-like claws pinning me. No one would ever find me down here.

"We're almost there. Well, if the superstitions are correct anyway."

He tightened his grip on my arm and dragged me forward again. The slope leveled out and the echo of our feet ceased. There was still no breeze, no airflow of any kind, but I knew that we were precariously close to a precipice. My mind conjured an image of a rickety wooden bridge, spanning a wide gulf. The rope holding up the edges frayed and clinging on by a single strand as it groaned and sagged under the weight of our bodies.

Though stranger still was the absence of any watching eyes. We were the only pieces of matter here—either alive, dead, or trapped somewhere undecided in between.

Dylan stopped suddenly and I froze next to him. His breathing was shallow, the only indication of his fear. In front of us, the darkness seemed to merge. An unseen force pulling all the particles of night together to form a pulsing void of cold energy.

"We're here. Ask it a question," he whispered.

I was still staring at it transfixed. My pulse beat in time with its ominous throb as if it was reaching out and squeezing my heart.

"Er, yeah. No, thanks," I whispered back.

His hand tightened on my arm. "Don't be afraid, just do it. Tell it who you are looking for?"

"You mean my father?"

"Yes, hurry up."

"Ouch!" There was a sharp pinch on my shoulder, and I leapt to the side, wrenching my arm free from Dylan.

I grabbed at the source of the pain and brushed my hand against the sharp hairs of the tarantula. I jumped again as Dylan's hand dug back into the flesh of my arm, pulling me back. His hand was hot fire against my chilled skin, and it burned as he gripped too tightly.

"Do it!" The growl reverberated around inside my head. Then more quietly, "I thought this is what you wanted?"

My stomach fell. Guilt. The most powerful motivational force. I took a shaky breath.

"Erm … is my father … down here?"

The void pulsed.

"You have to offer it something in return," Dylan whispered.

"Offer it what?"

Another pinch radiated up from my shoulder along with a furious clicking coming from Amura's mouth.

There was a soft rustle of fabric, and my other arm raised up slightly, which I presumed in the darkness to be a helpful shrug from Dylan.

Tired of being ignored, the spider stabbed at me again and then leapt off my shoulder. Two icy hands gripped me, and the scent of blood flowed into my nostrils as she spoke, face pressed uncomfortably close to mine.

"You don't make a deal with the gatekeeper, human. It will devour you and everything you have ever known or loved. Memories, emotions, everything that comprises your soul. Then it will spit you out, an empty vessel to inhabit this world for eternity."

It pulsed again behind her. A message formed in my mind, the letters jumbled as they tried to slot together like pieces in a jigsaw.

Give me the spider and you can have your father.

My heart jumped. So, he was down here. Trapped for years. That must be why he had never contacted me. The longing that I had tried to ignore for a decade pushed to the surface. Magnified due to the loneliness lying heavy on my heart since leaving that kitchen. Since realizing that the happy family life I had lived was just a charade.

It pulsed again.

She's already dead. I'll send him in her place.

"It wants you, Amura," I whispered.

"Are you in communication with it?" There was

an urgency in her usually calm voice.

"Just let her talk to it," Dylan said.

"You don't know what you are talking about. You're going to get her killed."

Snarl collided with snarl whilst the pulsing continued in front of me. It seemed to be expanding. Absorbing the tension, feeding off the fear.

I'll take you instead.

The pulsing was hypnotic. The vibrations rippled through my body. I needed to move toward it but the ice on my shoulders and fire on my arm had me trapped. It gave another frustrated surge of energy, and the room became clear before me. Everything was formed of squiggling black lines. The walls, the floor, the ceiling. It was all alive. My stomach heaved as I realized they were maggots.

They parted below our feet. Squirming to either side, opening a void that nothing could penetrate.

Dylan's hand wrenched free as he plummeted down into the dark. Amura still had me gripped by the shoulders, my sweater clenched between her fists.

But even her iron strength could not keep us in the air as the void opened its large mouth and swallowed us whole.

Chapter Twenty-One

I landed on a soft but uneven surface which reminded me of a lumpy mattress. Amura was still attached to my sweater. I couldn't see her, and she wasn't breathing or making any noise, but my skin chilled wherever she touched.

There was a dull pulse of light that briefly lit the space. My eyes roved wildly looking for where Dylan had fallen.

"Dyl—" I began to yell, but Amura slapped me hard, the sound echoing loudly.

I clutched at my throbbing cheek. It felt like I'd been hit with a brick. I got the message, but it was too late. The mattress beneath me started to swell, tilting and groaning before it relaxed again. Another pulse of light came, the rhythm like a slow heartbeat.

I still couldn't see him.

The mattress shifted again, and my foot fell between the soft folds. It was slimy and cold, and I immediately tried to pull it back up, but it was stuck. I gripped my leg with both hands and yanked hard, at the same time something strong and knobby closed around my ankle. Amura noticed and she wrenched my leg up just as another pulse beat. In the gloom a severed hand dangled from my foot, skeletal fingers gripping my ankle like a bracelet. I screamed and the mattress tilted violently.

Another pulse beamed out revealing that we were perched on a writhing heap of corpses. As the pulses became more regular, the bodies began to stir. Arms, legs and torsos tangled together stretched as far as I could see.

Amura dragged me to my feet, and I wobbled as my foot slipped again off the broad back I had been sitting on. Her cold hand gripped under my upper arm, and she pulled me forward. Another pulse shone showing the faint glow of auburn hair. Dylan was tangled in a mass of bodies, multiple bony arms encircling him and preventing him from crying out.

"Over there!"

Amura dug her nails into my flesh as punishment for speaking but it was too late. The words soared around the space, spurring the corpses into action. She sprinted away, dragging me behind. Bony hands gripped my clothes, fumbling for purchase of my skin underneath. The smell of decay was overpowering as we disturbed the rotting bodies. It shot out in geysers as small air pockets formed between the tangled corpses.

My foot slipped again, sliding off a large skull, the skin and hair degloving under my weight. Amura gave up dragging me and hoisted me up. Her arm tightened around my waist as she flew over the mass of bodies.

As we neared Dylan, she grabbed him by the front of his shirt and forced him to his feet. Snarling crackled through the air, and I caught glimpses of his body stretching and elongating as he transformed. He bounded after us and we slid down the side of the heap. A rumbling erupted like a great earthquake was following and Amura sprang onward, fortunately having given up on making me run, carrying me as easily as a doll.

"You need to control them, human!" she yelled.

"What?"

"Use your gift. It's easier to command the dead when they are just empty vessels, not inhabited by a soul."

"How am I supposed to do that? I'm not a me—"

"Figure it out or you and the werewolf die."

We slid to a stop. As another pulse flashed, a wall

loomed in front of us.

"There's no way out," Amura said. "Except back up the way we came."

I looked up into the black, unable to see anything. From behind us the rumbling intensified, interspersed with the scratching of nails and wet thumps as the corpses pressed on toward us.

"Take us one by one, Amura," Dylan snarled. He had transformed back into his human form, standing between me and the approaching bodies, fists clenched but eyes wide and nostrils flared. "It's my fault she is down here. I will hold them back. Take Anna now."

"No, there isn't time. They will kill you. Even as the werewolf, you are no match for them. You have to trust in her ability."

"Stop arguing and just go!" I snapped.

Another pulse. This time I could see the approaching wall of corpses. They were swarming over each other, tugging and clawing, a grotesque tangled mess. I pushed down the nausea as my stomach lurched.

I focused on the portal's signal—the pulsing message. I had to shut it down. I closed my eyes, stopped inhaling the rotting scent through my nose and stilled my shallow breaths. The vibrations filled my body. I sensed its urgency as the pulsing increased again. A tickling sensation washed over me like hundreds of tiny spiders crawling down my body and when I opened my eyes, I was viewing the scene from above.

A spark of electricity fired within my brain. For an instant, a millisecond so fleeting that I believed it to be true, I saw myself back in that box. Heard my screams and felt my body shudder as my fingernails carved panicked gutters in the wood inside. But I was *seeing* myself. Viewing from above, watching my father standing to the side, hammer in hand, intently staring at the wood. His face was not disgusted, not traumatized, but hopeful. Had he known what I could do?

I snapped back to the present. My body lay on the Chasm floor nestled against the wall. My hands were splayed and limbs stiff. Dylan hovered over me, his head whipping back and forth between me and the approaching corpses. His panicked breaths echoed, interrupted by a forlorn whine.

I focused back on the pulsing. Pushing with all my strength to force the signal back toward the portal. It faltered. It slid back a few feet, and the closest corpses slowed to a crawl.

"She's barely breathing! Her heart is too slow." Dylan's voice whined into the air again. "You need to get her out of here."

"You need to trust her. Trust me. Leave her and I'll take you!"

Dimly, I felt a flash of irritation. Why weren't they escaping? My lapse in concentration was immediately punished by the pulse rebounding. The intensity forced past my feeble blockage and the corpses slid toward us on the floor again.

Amura grabbed the back of Dylan's shirt and dragged him from my body on the floor. Her fingers sharpened into long piercing talons as she transformed into a large phoenix. She flapped frantically, Dylan growling and protesting as his feet thrashed in the air.

I focused again, sending my energy toward the signal. It wavered, but I couldn't force it back. The portal swelled in frustration, pouring all its energy back into the throbbing pulse, determined to overpower me.

"It's not working!" Dylan yelled from above. "They are getting closer. Amura, let me go."

An angry squawk answered him, and the talons ratcheted tighter, making him cry out again. Another surge of annoyance ran through me, breaking my concentration. The corpses surged forward again, groping blindly toward my immobile body on the floor.

The sound of wings returned as Amura dived back toward the ground. I tried to stop the pulse, tried to push back the signal. The portal's voice suddenly spoke to me.

Your father is still down here. Stop fighting and join him.

My hold broke.

I jerked back into my body, eyes snapping open. Sharp claws pierced my arms as jagged nails tore at my legs. I kicked out savagely, my foot connecting with a heavy torso. Gusts of stale air blew strongly into my face as the powerful wings above me began generating lift. Sagging gratefully, giving myself to her, I trusted in her power to hold me.

The pulsing below faded, gradually ceasing to beat and throwing me back into total darkness.

NK BROWN

Chapter Twenty-Two

The scent of rot and decay faded, lingering only on my clothes and ironed into the creases of my skin. As we reached the bridge, Amura released her hold and I fell to the floor, my knees cracking on the stone. I lay there, unable to see anything, as helpless as a newborn. My whole body drained from the exertion.

Breath whispered hot in my face, and I pulled away with a start.

"I'm sorry, Anna. I just…" He didn't finish the sentence. He growled impatiently and I pictured him kneeling beside me, tearing at his hair, a grimace lining his face. Trying again, he whispered, "You got your army of the dead after all, though."

Groaning, I shook my head at him. I tried to push him away, but he hardly budged. "It wasn't my army. I was just trying to stop them."

"It was really impressive." He leaned in further, his body heat washing over me. "You were *controlling* them."

"There are three passageways ahead," Amura's voice broke in. "We don't have time to sit here and apologize or discuss what just happened. If we fail this zone, we get trapped down here."

His powerful hand grasped mine and he pulled me to my feet. He let go but stood just off my shoulder, breathing down my neck.

"So which way is it, Amura?" I asked.

"I don't know, human. I was distracted on the way down trying to work out what crazy scheme the werewolf was hatching."

Great. "Dylan, do you remember?"

"We came downward."

Shit. "Can't you, like, smell your way back or something?" I asked.

He snorted. I raised my shoulder reflexively as his breath tickled my neck.

"No, I can't 'smell my way back'."

I crossed my arms over my chest, and he added quickly, "The lack of air flow down here just makes everything smell the same. Like decay. And death."

"Lovely. So, I suppose we should just guess and hope then?"

I meant it as a joke. When neither of them said anything, I cursed again. A faint light appeared in the central tunnel. There was no sound as it approached, the naked feet silently grazing the floor. In the light of a burning torch, the sculpted body of a man appeared. Its brown torso was bare, muscles rippling in the flickering light.

Gradual warmth fell upon me as the rays of light licked my face. He stood still at the entrance to the central passageway. As he raised the torch higher in front of him, his face appeared. Small, triangular ears were perched high upon a furred head. A glistening nose sniffed the air at the end of a narrow muzzle.

He seemed to be scenting something, head cocked to the side as the doleful chocolate brown eyes turned to each of us in turn. Lowering the torch, he gestured up the middle tunnel. Hidden sconces within the dark walls caught fire with a uniform swoosh. The light streamed out toward me, and I sighed with relief. I almost didn't care what would happen next, if I wasn't condemned to blindness anymore.

My feet moved toward the light.

"What are you doing?" Dylan growled, reaching out and pulling me back.

"We should follow."

"Absolutely not."

"He's going to guide us back."

"How do you know that, human?" Amura asked, a note of suspicion in her voice.

I shrugged. "Well, he's less scary than the corpses and at least I can see how I am going to die if we go that way."

Dylan growled.

I rolled my eyes at him in response.

Prizing his hands off me, I walked toward the strange figure. Dylan remained hot on my heels. Amura leapt into the air and the fluttering of leathery wings returned as the flying fox circled around our heads.

The guide noted our response and turned slowly. We followed, our footsteps softly reverberating around us. I became attuned to my body—my heart squeezing painfully in my chest, the tug of aching muscles in my calves and then the throbbing that resumed its attack on my injured shoulder. We must have walked for miles or in large circles, the only indication of any progress being the gradual slope of the floor and a slight pressure in my ears.

The tunnel eventually ended as we entered a large antechamber. The guide raised his hand and another whoosh rang out as the flames erupted around the room. It was still dimly lit, the sconces high on the dark walls and the flickering light made the shadows dance and writhe in the corners. In the center of the room an object hovered. The guide gestured with his thin, tanned hand and Dylan and I crept uncertainly toward it.

"Where's the way out?" he whispered.

"Well, I don't know." I looked around. "Your eyes are better than mine. Can you see anything?"

A door slid across the opening to the tunnel we had just left and clicked shut. The air stiffened around me, and the familiar edge of panic crept in as my mind flashed to images it conjured up frequently against my will. Of small airless coffins as I tried to claw and scrabble my way out. Always unsuccessfully. Always ending with broken fingernails stuck in the thick walls, blood seeping down the claw marks as the blackness enveloped me...

Sensing my fear, Dylan gripped my hand. It was too tight as he crushed my fingers in his, but I appreciated the distraction. The guide was standing like a sentinel next to the floating object, waiting for us to proceed. The baleful eyes watched us dully.

A black feather appeared in the air and floated noiselessly down, landing on a small silver tray. It was on one side of a weighing scales. The simple needle in the center pointed toward the feather. An empty tray waited expectantly, raised up in the air on the other side.

"Amura," I whispered toward the ceiling, unsure where she was hiding, "you're going to have to be the one to do to this."

"I can do it," Dylan said.

"No, you're too big."

He looked at me quizzically.

A quick breeze circulated around us and then Amura's slender figure with flame red hair materialized.

"What do I have to do, human?"

"The guide needs us to complete the test so he can let us through to the Chasm."

She narrowed her black eyes at me. "That is just an old superstition. It is probably just a trick by this demon."

"Well, that's what he wants."

"How can you possibly know that?"

"It's obvious."

"I told you," Dylan growled, "I'll do it."

"And I told you, you can't." I couldn't stop the annoyance in my voice. "It needs to be lighter than the feather to pass through. That's how the story goes anyway. My father used to read it to me when I was young. It was actually pretty terrifying, which is how it stuck in my memory for so long."

"What's the story then?"

"Once upon a time…" I began.

Amura sprang over to me and halted, her face uncomfortably close to mine. "Quicker."

"Erm, okay." I swallowed then began again, "Once upon a time…"

Dylan snorted next to me. Amura's lips curled, exposing her pointed teeth. I ploughed on regardless.

"Once upon a time, there was a young girl who lived in a beautiful palace, nestled in the heart of a magical forest. She had everything her heart could want. Food, clothes, friends. But what she really wanted was to be magical. She longed to soar like the eagles or flow like the rivers, taking whichever shape she fancied. There was an old wives' tale her maid would often tell that those who consumed the flesh of an innocent magical being would absorb its powers. But in doing so, the creature would die and be doomed to spend its days endlessly scouring the shadow world, trying to retrieve its stolen magic.

"The idea consumed her, taking over every part of her life. She knew the creature she would use. There was a small, furry monster that often snuck into the kitchen at night, searching desperately for the tiniest of crumbs to fill its hollow, aching belly. Its long bushy tail would leave faint marks of soot like the winding trail of a snake in the sand, leading into and out of the old fireplace. The girl began to leave small morsels of food out every night. Each time placing it closer to a small alcove where she could lie in wait.

"The creature was tentative at first. Snatching at the food and fleeing back into the night. But gradually it became more confident, eventually remaining in place to finish its meal before returning to its lair.

"The girl waited in the alcove one night, a large dagger in her hand. As the narrow twitching snout bent down toward the temptation she had laid, she sprang at it. The dagger sliced deeply into the skin at the base of its tail. The creature screamed in pain, red eyes flashing and tried to run, but it was pinned to the floor. Its long claws scrabbled desperately on the stone and there was a loud ripping sound, as its tail detached from its body. It shrieked in desperation as the severed part of it twitched helplessly and then, turning, it bolted back up the chimney and into the night.

"The young girl released the writhing tail and clutched it tight. She felt not an ounce of pity for the wretched creature whose magic she had stolen. She threw it into a large cauldron bubbling on the fire and the smell of stewed meat filled the air. Mouth watering, she boiled it with the finest delicacies she could find and went to bed full and satisfied.

"Later that night, she awoke with a start. She was sweating and the silken sheets were tangled around her. Thinking it must be the magic working she laid her head down once more but then an eerie voice wafted around the room and her eyes snapped open again. It was as if the wind itself was speaking. Searching for its magic soul. She could see nothing, except the dying embers of the fire so she closed her eyes again. The wind whispered again and then again, every minute becoming more and more agitated. As the last of the red glow faded from the charred remains of the fire, the room fell into darkness.

"A heavy weight sprang onto the bed. She sat bolt

upright and pulled the sheets high under her chin, eyes wide but unseeing. She felt it creeping up her feet, to her legs and it settled on her lap. The red eyes blinked wide, and one final warning was whispered, '*Give me back my soul.*'

"Terrified, the girl cried 'I don't have it! It's gone.' The red eyes blinked again and then it sprang at her, trapping her on the bed as it ripped and tore at her stomach. The girl shrieked and cried out for help but then finally lay still, as the creature fished out its tail. Before it could flee back up the chimney, the door banged open, and the angry guards barged in. They caught the creature and killed it. Burning its body with its beloved tail so that it would never come back to haunt them again."

"How is that relevant to us?" Dylan whispered, but I could sense his absorption in the story as his grip on my hand tightened further.

"I haven't finished it yet," I replied.

Amura pursed her lips together, but didn't say anything, so I plowed on.

"Both the girl and the creature were sent down to purgatory. They had to be sorted by the spirits and pass a series of tests before their souls would be allowed to continue their journey. The girl passed all the tests easily, she was young and naïve and told a woeful tale of the wrongful attack and murder by the creature. The creature in return said nothing in its defense.

"The gatekeeper announced there would only be one soul to pass on, the other destined to be trapped forever. He produced two identical sets of silver scales. On each of the dishes, he placed a downy feather.

"*To pass through the gates, your soul must be pure. It must be lighter than the feather. Your sins erased by the goodness within.*'

"He reached his clawed hand into the chest of the

girl and pulled out her still heart. He reached toward the creature, but it spoke a request first. *'Take my tail. That is where my soul lies, not my heart.'* So, the gatekeeper took the severed tail. He placed one on each scale and whilst the girl's heart dropped like a stone, the tail rested lightly, perfectly balanced against the feather. The creature turned to the girl and gave a toothy sneer. He knew she had boiled and eaten all the meat, leaving only the furry carcass behind. With that, the creature passed onto the afterlife and the girl was condemned."

Amura's expression was incomprehensible. Dylan still looked confused.

"So?" he said.

"So," I said with a sigh, "isn't it obvious?"

I turned back to Amura and lowered my voice so no sound would travel to the guide's ears, "What is the smallest creature you can be?"

She said nothing but melted from my view. The buzzing sound of miniscule wings appeared in front of me, the red throat of the hummingbird catching in the torch light. She flew toward the guide and hovered. The slow, tanned hand came forward and sliced open her feathery chest using one razor sharp nail. He placed the immobile heart, black and glistening, on the opposing tray and the balance shifted. The needle shot past the halfway point toward the tiny heart then flew back again, vibrating indecisively.

It finally settled perfectly in the center.

Chapter Twenty-Three

There was no reaction from the guard's sorrowful eyes. His hands dutifully returned the heart to its position, and he turned in the direction of the opposing wall. Another door silently slid open, and an inky-black tunnel emerged. No lights graced us this time, but undeterred, Dylan pulled me forward quickly. Amura spread her wings and stretched out of the tiny hummingbird. She resumed her icy grip on my shoulder and, sandwiched between them, we all made for the exit.

The tunnel lurched sharply upward, and I fell forward, my knee banging against a hard obstruction. The two hands on either side prevented me from reaching the ground as I was dragged upright again, whilst my knee throbbed angrily.

"Sorry," Dylan whispered. "Steps."

I picked up my feet higher, half-stumbling, half-carried by the two of them and we made it to the top. The familiar flicker of spirits emerged around us again, bringing with it the unnerving feeling of being watched and judged by unseen beings.

The moment my eyes caught the faint shimmer of long hair in the flickering red light up ahead, my ears picked up the impatient sigh. Amura's icy hand on my arm disappeared and the tiny scurrying legs crawled back up my arm.

"You wimp," I muttered.

She clicked a laugh at me in response.

We neared the others. Chris folded his arms tightly across his chest, the edges of his shirt flapping around him as the wind blustered.

"What did I tell you, girl?"

Dylan cut her off with a growl. "It wasn't her

fault. It was my idea."

"What you need to remember, *wolf*, is that she is just a human. She is not special. She is not powerful. She is from a race that feels the only way to protect themselves is to ostracize anything that is different." The wind continued to rustle angrily around us, probing for answers. "Although the spider here, after your little adventure, thinks she may be able to harness her medium powers. That does increase her value further, no?"

"We need to hurry up and finish this thing or we are going to run out of time," Chris said, "and it will be *your* fault." His brown eyes flashed in my direction.

There was no point rolling my eyes at him in the murky darkness, but I did it anyway.

This time as we walked, Pixie and Chris hemmed me in like security guards worried about a high flight risk prisoner. Dylan was forced to walk behind, and the low, throaty grumble echoed around us, merging with our hollow footsteps.

It wasn't long before we halted again. This time because our way ahead was blocked. Multiple flickering flames in an array of different hues formed a loose semi-circle. They tightened quickly around us like a noose. Dylan's strong form squeezed in beside me and the wind blew loudly in annoyance.

Different voices began talking in my head. Some were too fast to understand, some in languages I did not know.

"Save me. I need to return to watch over my children..."

Next to me, Chris stopped and was squeezing his hands tightly over his ears, back bent in an effort to ease the pain in his head. Dylan was suffering a similar fate and ground his teeth together, one hand digging into my waist, the other clenched into a fist.

"Release me, girl. The world will not know what hit it. There is still so much destruction to cause…"

The voices grew louder, more demanding.

"If you do not free me, I will haunt you and everyone you have ever known or loved for the rest of your miserable existence…"

Pleas, threats, horrific stories were all screamed into my mind. Dylan clutched at me, his heart pounding against my shoulder.

"Don't trust the man, he works for the government. Don't trust the government, they do not work for you. Don't trust the man…"

Somewhere nearby Pixie began an incantation. A warm breeze circled around us, tossing loose curls of my hair. As the warmth increased, the voices faded, and I chanced a glance up. The flickering shapes pressed closer. Cutting off any escape. They weren't touching us, but the urgency was still present. Their desperation made my throat tight, and my tongue stick to the roof of my mouth as I tried to swallow.

Only one could leave and they knew it.

"Pick one spirit and let's go!" Pixie yelled at us, her face contorted in an effort to keep the voices at bay.

This was my only chance to save my father. I scanned the Chasm, the multi-colored flames pressing all around, but none were familiar. My soul did not lurch in any one direction because I knew, deep down, who really deserved to be freed.

"Which one?" I asked.

The blue one over there. Open your mind. The rest will come naturally.

"Okay." I went to walk out of the circle of warmth.

Dylan grabbed my arm and pulled me back. "You don't know what you are doing. Let me do it. It may be dangerous." He hissed at me with the curl of a snarl, his voice unable to stay at a whisper.

"It's okay. I trust them." Swallowing hard, I crept forward, Dylan's fingers reluctantly sliding from my arm.

The moment I stepped out of the magic the air around me froze. Shivers assaulted my body, and the voices tormented my mind once again. Another flash of memory hit. My father sat on my bed, pen scratching the words of my dream. 'Compartmentalize, Anna,' he said, 'then you can hear each individual voice'.

"They need me! They cannot live without me..."

I kept focused on the sky-blue flame.

"I will haunt you, possess you, destroy you, unless..."

Thought about the young girl with the blue eyes.

"Don't trust the man, he works for the government. Don't trust the government, they do not work for you. Don't trust the man..."

Thought about the silver locket.

"Selfish girl, thinking only of yourself..."

Thought about the life their daughter and Johannes were never able to experience.

"Don't I matter? Am I not enough..."

Thought about the day I lost my own father.

I will be whoever you want me to be. Just save me..."

Thought about the strength of a parent's love.

I held my arms out in front of me and opened my palms. The blue flame licked at my fingertips, the touch like warm waves on a sandy beach. Then it rolled up my body. Every emotion spilled into me as if it were my own. The devastation. The grief. The never-ending hope. I understood the decision to save this spirit. To allow them an eternity of happiness that was taken from them in their first life. The first step of righting an injustice.

"Goodbye, Johannes," I choked into the black air. "Go unite with her in the afterlife."

Johannes left my body and ascended.

The red flame of the spirit flickered. I had come to enjoy their presence, their choice to speak through me provided unexpected comfort during this ordeal, but most importantly I knew they had suffered more than I ever would. They guttered and dimmed. They had burned so strongly for such a long time that the relief was palpable.

And I felt no regret at putting their happiness above my own.

NK BROWN

Chapter Twenty-Four

"Memories are powerful. They shape who we are, who we will become and why we will never change. Time to get to know your teammates before the final challenge." I repeated the words as they appeared in my mind.

I was emotionally exhausted. Physically exhausted. I didn't want to be a pawn in this game anymore. It was as if someone heard my plea. The homely kitchen materialized around me. The pristine ceiling fan wafted the smell of crackling bacon around the small room. The old cuckoo clock gleamed on the wall, someone had replaced the paint, and it shone with fresh varnish. The straight hands hovered just before midday.

Sitting down at the empty chair, I stretched my arms out in the wide expanse next to me. I was starving. My mouth was watering, my stomach grumbling. I looked over at my father. His grey eyes were concerned. His face barely holding onto the smile I loved so much. Curly brown hair was randomly arranged on his head, no attempt made to control it. Everybody said I was the spitting image of him. That I looked nothing like my mother. This suited me just fine.

There was a swooshing sound as the three cylinders around the room disappeared. I'd forgotten. Today was the experiment. The first day I was old enough to vote. An alarm began to sound from somewhere in the repressed area of my hippocampus.

The clock on the wall tolled. The little peasant figure shot out and started enthusiastically chopping the wood, perfectly in sync with the dirge. The forced smile on my father's lips dropped away as my mother lightly touched his hand and bowed her head, ready to repeat the words she had always said to us.

"Let us offer thanks as a family. For those who have valiantly tried and failed in the many years past and for those that are destined to fight and die for us tomorrow, so that we may all live in unity. All entities together in a peaceful world. Until death do us part."

Until death do us part. The words were etched into my mind, carved into my throat but no sound emerged.

Perhaps if I didn't speak, it would end differently.

Another cylinder appeared in the corner of the room. It was empty except for a sprinkling of small red stars at the bottom. As I watched, more stars slowly showered down from above, twinkling and spinning as they descended to the bottom.

A loud knock sounded at the door.

My heart stopped. My head snapped around. The alarm in my brain was becoming shrill. I just couldn't grasp the memory.

The door opened and four large security guards burst in. All had annihilators clasped in strong, haired hands. All pointing directly at my father. I leapt up and started to scream. The memory burst into the forefront of my mind. I had lived through this once before and I was not going to let it happen again. I lunged toward the door, but a familiar hand clamped down over my mouth and an arm wound around my chest, dragging me back.

"The girl cannot interfere." The voice like the wind whispered around me.

"It's not real. Stop and think. It's not real." The words came out as a snarl as Dylan fought to keep me still.

"It. Is. Real!" I screamed.

The red stars were accelerating. They were

gushing into the cylinder, filled over halfway. The security guards entered the room and encircled my father. Two of them had the square black muzzles of the annihilators trained directly at his heart. The other two snatched at his sleeves, dragging him up out of the chair, the screeching of the wood protesting over the tiled floor.

I bit down hard on the hand over my mouth, my teeth sinking into the soft flesh. Ignoring the yelp of pain, I lurched toward them.

This time I was thrown backward and pinned into the chair. My head snapped back, and my spine crunched against the hard wood.

I gripped the edges of the table, knuckles white. There was a slow dripping from one of the hands pinning my shoulders, the drips splashed as they landed on my leg. All I could do was watch, frozen with horror, as the slight figure of my father was dragged toward the door, overpowered and unresisting. My nails carved deep grooves into the hard wood of the table that no amount of polish would ever fix.

The cylinder was full. The stars kept pouring in, the seams bulging with the strain. Spiderwebs fractured up the glass, popping as they stretched. A rush of air swooped out as the thing exploded. Thousands of dagger-like projections shot into the air, swarming toward us.

If I hadn't been restrained in my seat, if I had run like my body wanted me to, I never would have seen it. As the stars poked and needled and buried into my flesh, blocking out the light and turning everything blood red, I saw the corners of my mother's mouth twitch.

The smile I should never have seen.

NK BROWN

Chapter Twenty-Five

A jolt, as if suspended on the end of bungee line, a barb snagging a fish, pulled me into another room. I couldn't focus. The hatred pounded through my veins— the edges of my vision swam. The anger was all consuming, but I was one wrong breath away from inconsolable grief. Very slowly, questions began to link up with answers in my mind.

In front of me, Chris sat nervously on a straight-backed chair. His filthy white shirt and torn leather trousers looked woefully out of place in the immaculate office. His leg bounced up and down, tapping a crazy rhythm on the polished marble floor. Floor to ceiling windows stretched along the back of the office, a vast moorland stretching out to the horizon.

Behind a huge transparent desk, sat a petite woman. Her grey hair was scraped back into a bun, face unnaturally smooth for her age. She sat deathly still, the steady rise and fall of her chest the only indication she was even alive.

The old lady cleared her throat. "Thank you for joining me today, Mr. Childerley. As you know it is time for the annual reviews. Your position within our government will be determined after this interview and with it your standing in the lottery."

Chris squirmed within his seat. The sporadic tapping of his foot set my teeth on edge. I dug my broken fingernails into my palms trying to force myself to concentrate. In the corner of the room the familiar cylinder appeared, and the red stars began trickling down.

The lady continued, "We'll start with your excellent work for the lottery broadcasts. Your piece on why vampires will never be able to integrate within a civilized society was truly groundbreaking. The scientific evidence you found, proving they were missing a large section of their prefrontal cortex, making them incapable of demonstrating any kind of impulse control is going to be a hit. We plan to show it alongside them losing said control in the experiments and we should have plenty of opportunities for this as you know."

I know why my mother was so desperate to find another partner after they took my father away. One vote each, no way to stack the odds.

"How many vampires did you have to experiment on before you could safely conclude your research?"

Chris whispered, "Eighty-six."

A soft rattle began behind my ear where the rattlesnake had coiled itself, dusty red scales scratching my skin as the vibrations started. Chris turned around in his chair and mouthed, "It's not real," but his wide eyes and sweat-soaked brow told another story.

She continued, "Well, good riddance I say. After this piece airs we may even be able to exclude all the vampires from the Undead Government. One less sect to contend with. Without them, the others of the party are going to struggle." She gave a small, impressed nod.

I know why she cooked bacon at every lottery, even after he left. She thought it was my favorite, too.

"Secondly, your collaboration with Mr. Middleton on the proposal to increase the survival of humans within the experiment was very interesting. Your want for equality and diversity between the entrants is very noble. We have discussed an alteration of this theme at the quarterly meeting. You should commend yourself that a variation of your novel idea is going to form the basis of a new teamwork structure in the upcoming experiment. It will certainly count in your favor should you ascend the ladder here within our government. Especially, if it works." She gave a sly smile, no wrinkles gathering at the corner of her upturned mouth.

I know why Drew felt so guilty that day.

The stars were halfway up the cylinder but still filling slowly. Chris stopped trying to look over at us. His eyes kept darting between the woman's face and the corner of her desk. He seemed unsure about what was about to come. The rattling in my ear reverberated around in my head and I pressed hard on my temples to try and massage away the noise.

"Now, there is something I would like you to see, before we proceed." The old lady's voice was sharp and an edge of danger had crept into it. She pressed a section of her desk, and a large translucent screen folded up from the edge. She nodded at it, held up two fingers and the screen buzzed to life.

A smoky, seedy bar appeared on the screen. The lacquered counter hosted a variety of people, glasses in hand, heads pressed together in loud conversation as they fought to be heard over the loud thrum of the bass. The floor glistened in places, where unknown substances clung to it, eagerly waiting to grab hold of the sole of an unsuspecting shoe.

In the corner of the room, Chris was seated at a small table. His straight nose and brown eyes were the only familiar features in an otherwise enchanted expression. His barely touched drink was sitting a fraction away from his manicured hand, which inched hopefully across the table toward his companion.

The screen zoomed in further and over the loud background music the sound of two voices filtered into the room. His companion had short black hair woven delicately around her head, so perfectly coiffured that it looked stolen from a mannequin. Her silky sea-green dress clung to her slim figure, holding the attention of many admirers in the crowded bar. Chris was gazing rapt into her purple eyes. His mouth was slightly parted and his whole body leaned toward her like he was being pulled by an invisible string.

"The information you provided us so far has been very useful, my dear." The voice crept like moonlight, rhythmic but secretive. "But we need more, my love, yes?" Her delicate hand slid across the table and rested on his. "We have the same goals, you and I. The only way to be together is to unite the beings, destroy the fences and disband the government. The only barriers are in the upper echelons of the Human Government. They don't want unity. They don't want peace. They want to keep two souls who are made for each other, like us, apart for eternity."

She leaned into him, the purple eyes flashing momentarily to black. She kissed him softly, just long enough to draw him closer, not long enough to satisfy.

"You should propose a change to the lottery drawing system, my dear. Propose that all humans are eligible, maybe that more should be selected to increase the odds of survival, no? If you can make it so that all levels of the government can be selected from, then we can make sure that certain individuals, those standing in the way of our love, are chosen."

Chris edged further toward her, the corners of his mouth turning down as he smiled at her. "I'll do anything so we can be together."

She smiled back at him, a triumphant gleam in her purple eyes and she kissed him gently again, securing the promise.

The screen went black and quietly folded back into the desk. The keen gaze of the old woman had not left Chris's face throughout the video and there was now a malicious energy emanating from her still figure.

I know how I won the vote. It was four to one.

'So, Mr. Childerley," she smiled widely, "due to your exemplary record here in the government, we are going to excuse your gullibility. The other beings are always looking for a chink in the armor, a way to exploit our trusting and kind nature. Due to this we are not going to arrest nor execute you." She licked her plump, scarlet lips and her body moved forward by a millimeter. "Instead, you will be the volunteer candidate from the government this year to enter the lottery. I think all the work you have done so far should give you an advantage, and if you win…" She raised a manicured eyebrow on a forehead stretched so tight you could almost see her skull. "I will give you my place on the senior council."

The cylinder exploded, pelting us with the sharp reminders of the past. I was left with only one remaining question.

Why?

NK BROWN

Chapter Twenty-Six

When the red haze cleared, I found myself standing in another kitchen. The vast domed ceiling stretched up and into the sky. The sun directly overhead poured through the large sunroof, filling the space with light and warmth. The pristine granite countertops sparkled as rays of sunlight bounced off them. Not a speck of dust could be seen anywhere. The walls shone with a rich cream hue, adding to the brightness of the space. The spicy smell of cinnamon and clove filled my nostrils and made my heart squeeze.

Along the walls were hung many framed pictures. There were also quotations, bold against the neutral colors of the paint that screamed their messages to any who glanced their way. The one closest to me read 'we are the pure bloods'.

Next to it was a photograph depicting a large man with almond-shaped eyes and spiked auburn hair. He was standing framed by a chain link fence. Two younger men stood either side of him, both spitting images—neither were old enough yet to have the red stubble lining their strong jaws. I recognized the one on the left instantly.

All three stood proud, with wide grins, pointed canine teeth glinting from the flash of the camera. In the large man's hands was the severed head of a young girl. The flesh hung from her neck in shreds, blood coating the man's jeans and pooling on the floor beneath him. Her blonde hair was tangled and knotted in his split knuckles, her face streaked with dirt. Even in death her face told a story of abject terror.

A soft, bubbling wail filled the room. It was muffled, held back through scarlet-tipped, perfectly manicured fingernails. Smooth, blonde hair framed a beautiful face with honey-colored eyes that shone with sadness as she shook quietly in the corner. Sitting stiffly at an expansive mahogany table in the center of the room were two young boys. They looked to be about eight and ten, similar to the boys in the photograph but they still held an aura of innocence about them. Both were quivering, their mother's distress causing them to fidget and twitch in the silk backed chairs. Soft whines escaped their lips.

It was then that I noticed Dylan. He was sitting next to the two boys at the clean table. I expected him to react to the scene, to pace about, to show some kind of recollection of the memory playing out in front of him. Looking closer, fine tendrils were wrapped around his torso. They were pulsating, alive, and had him immobilized, carving into his bulging muscles as he strained against them. Another was wrapped around his mouth, stifling the growls and snarls coming from deep within his chest.

I didn't want to know what was coming. But I watched, helpless, transfixed, my heart pounding in my throat, breaths shallow and strained in the richly scented air.

Heavy footsteps marched toward the house, becoming progressively louder. The sobbing decreased to barely controlled whimpers, and the younger boys froze, their fingers clasped tightly in their laps. Both were staring fixedly at a point on the far wall. Directly opposite the head of the table, there was a section with neat, black slashes carved into it. Four names were neatly printed next to each column: Dylan, Damon, Donnie and David.

The door to the kitchen flew open crashing against the wall, causing shards of cream to plunge to the floor. The woman pressed herself further into the corner, streaks of mascara running down her ashen face. The man in the photo filled the doorway. A vein throbbed in the center of his forehead and his eyes narrowed as he scanned the room. One giant hand gripped the edge of the doorframe, the screech of his nails filling the air as he carved out fresh grooves in the immaculate surface.

He strode over to the far wall and stabbed the final line on the longest tally. Painfully slow, he turned back around. An oppressive silence sucked the life out of the sunny kitchen.

His thin lips curled back over bared teeth as he tore up a handwritten letter he had been clutching in one hand. The ripping echoed through the still air, each jagged shred floating slowly to the floor.

"The Demi Government has offered me a pathetic deal," he snarled, eyes flashing as he looked around the room. "They took Damon and now they're punishing me again by taking Dylan." His stare bored into the huddled form at the table, still bound tightly, his every fiber fighting the restraints. "And after I have been doing their fucking job for them!"

He slammed his fist onto the table. The two younger boys jumped in their seats, hands still clutched tightly in their laps for support.

"Here is what you are going to do, boy," he spat at Dylan. "Go and enter that stupid lottery. Play the game, toe the line. Act every part of the sniveling, spineless creature they want us to be. You are going to be paired with a girl, I made it part of the deal. It won't be difficult to make her fall in love with you, humans are weak and are always attracted to what they don't deserve. You make everyone believe you've changed, that you are sorry for the impressive number of killings you racked up over the years, that you can coexist with *them*," he infused the word with decades' worth of hatred, "and they won't rip the family apart. You understand?"

I hadn't noticed the cylinder filling up in the corner of the room. Its glass edges groaned with the pressure.

"When you get back, we'll release Damon and go make up for all the lost time. Finish our duty to the werewolves. And, if you die," he paused. There was a sudden silence as the sob caught in the woman's throat huddled in the corner. "Then take as many of them out with you whilst you can."

The wails burst out of the woman's mouth as the cylinder exploded. The stars showered down around the room, stabbed into the framed photos, obscured the incendiary text on the walls.

This time I welcomed the burn as they tunneled into my flesh, turning everything around me red.

Chapter Twenty-Seven

The invisible cord snatched around my waist, jerking me into another scene. I knew this was a test designed to tear us apart so that we wouldn't complete the experiment. But I also knew what I had seen was the truth. Maybe Chris was right all along. He had never seen anything in me. What was there to see?

You need to focus, Anna. Pay attention.

Easier said than done. My mind was replaying the scene over and over. The words, the promise, the debt he owed. The spiky tail of the rattlesnake smacked into my face, and she hissed in my ear from the other side. I channeled my frustrations back into digging holes in my palms. The sharp pain necessary to keep my brain from stampeding off into the wild like a fleeing mustang, determined to let the panic drive it toward self-preservation.

We were standing in a graveyard. It was late winter, the somber trees were bare, a miserable permafrost still clinging onto any available surface. There was no moon and there were no stars. The dusky twilight enveloped everything within its cold fingers, leaving ominous shadows sporadically littering the crevices, with no prediction as to where they would reach.

The chill penetrated my thin layers, and I clenched my jaw shut to stop the knocking of my teeth, afraid to wake the dead from their slumber.

The gravestones closest to me were arranged in a circle around a large hewn stump, the tree having rotted long ago, leaving a centerpiece that reminded you all living things died. Even the trees were not immune to the hew of Death's scythe. Six figures, three female and three male, were seated on tombstones surrounding the deceased stump.

Pixie was perched delicately on a tall, thin grey stone. The bust of an angel protruded from the top and she was sitting carelessly on the crowned head, bare feet resting on the angel's open palms. Opposite her, was the faint glow and open face of the gold team's pixie. He was standing in front of a battered Celtic cross, the marbled surface pockmarked with black mold and stubborn green moss.

Two of the beings I didn't recognize. A young boy with dark skin, dark hair and eyes that almost glowed in the dim light. He was opposite an old woman. She was hunched over with wrinkled hands that gripped the smooth surface of the plain headstone she rested upon. Her neck curved out from under a thick woolen cape like a turkey vulture peering around for carrion. The old woman must be a witch of some kind. I had seen pictures in books at school. The older the appearance, the more damage had been done over the years. She must have been particularly powerful and senior within the ranks.

As she was opposite the young boy, I guessed he was a faerie. They could possess any human body that suited their purpose. An innocent child would be the perfect vessel. If this was a meeting of the magical council, then the last two positions would be held by elves.

The male and female elf were the only two of the same species sitting next to each other. Their hands were clasped gently together, a serene look on both their faces as they silently studied the others. Appearances like that were acutely deceptive. They were the two most powerful and foreboding figures there.

The strange part of this meeting was that they were in a well-tended cemetery. A *human* burial ground. There were no partitions, no fences, no regard for the rules separating the entities from each other. I bet the groundskeeper and many mourners probably passed over this very earth most days, picking up weeds, tending to the scraggly plants and laying flowers.

How much of a crossover between the beings occurred without our knowledge?

The memory had started midway through a heated debate. Snatches of the conversation were muffled by angry bursts of the wind, purposely interfering with the dialogue.

"The humans have no intention of a merger any time soon," the calm, sunny voice of the gold pixie spoke out, "and we in the forests are content with this. It is better for all our races if they continue to think that we are abiding by the laws and keeping ourselves separate."

"That is an outdated view, no?" Pixie argued. "The new wing wants the unity to occur, we have…" her words were obscured by a loud gust roaring in my ears, "and a seat at the Unified Government."

"The new wing is nothing but rebels and anarchists, they do not speak for the majority of us and neither do you."

"We are fading, we are being slowly picked off one by one and if we want to strengthen our hold within…" another gust blared, and I glared at her, of course she took no notice, "and put an end to the fighting, an end to the experiment, then we need to act now, yes?"

Amura rattled her tail in my ear, the extra noise not helping as I strained to listen to the parts Pixie didn't want us to hear.

"We want the merger too," the faerie said, the chirpy voice of the young boy out of place amongst the dismal graves. "We are running out of bodies to inhabit, and our choices are becoming…" he made a sweeping motion down his body, "desperate."

"The elves want access to the human population, no?" Pixie asked the two figures still holding hands on identical crumbling headstones.

They both nodded, the female's lips parted in a sneer, her hand tightening around her partner's. I didn't know why the elves wanted 'access' and I was pretty sure ignorance was bliss in this case.

"I have a source currently working on a…" I tried to watch her lips form the words as she obscured them, but she turned her head slightly, her shimmering hair covering the side of her face, "he is our hope of amalgamation. It is likely he will be punished and sent into the lottery if discovered and if that happens, I will go in to lead him through."

"That is the wrong choice for our species—"

"It is the only choice for our species."

The two of them paused, purple eyes flashing black across the broken stump separating them.

"I think a better option," the aged, wizened voice of the witch broke the silence, "is for both of you to enter." Her chapped lips broke into a strained grin, yellow teeth protruding from a rotten mouth. Her rancid breath lingered in the air, making my stomach churn. She continued, "The outcome will determine the fate of the Magic Government."

The young boy nodded in agreement, eyes shining with narcissistic excitement. The two elves inclined their heads in unison.

The decision was made.

The memory was ending, I turned to see the cylinder behind us almost full. Dylan was watching me intently. His gaze lingered even when I glanced away, making my skin prickle. He stood slightly back from me and Chris, who was glued to the scene in front taking no notice of anything else. I wanted to ignore him, to turn back without giving him any attention, but my eyes betrayed me, and they strayed to his face.

His expression could only be described as haunted. The guilt hung from the downturned corners of his mouth, shadows pressing heavily beneath his wounded eyes. He made no move to bridge the gap between us, but I could sense his longing to be close.

I didn't want him anywhere near me.

I turned back to the front, edging slightly closer to Chris as I did, knowing full well the effect this would have on him. The guilt barely touched me, the hurt was still too raw. I had done everything his father had bragged about. Fallen for his charm with ease. Allowed his intensity to make me feel alive. To feel wanted.

Just a gullible human after all.

NK BROWN

Chapter Twenty-Eight

"You have the council meeting tonight, Princess."

A young girl gently tipped water from an ornate porcelain bowl into the soil of a large Venus fly trap. Its long green spears lay open, the exposed pink heart warm and inviting. The water trickled in, the soil gurgling greedily as it sucked up the moisture. She raked at the uneven earth with her pale fingers and then smoothed it down, so that no wrinkle marred its brown surface. She kept her green eyes lowered and focused on her work, a shyness present in every hesitant movement.

The large room was filled with an abundance of life. Everywhere I looked there was something beautiful to see. The floor was adorned with delicate flowers and neatly trimmed shrubs, each branch perfectly shorn into the shapes of rushing waves or floating clouds. Vines bursting with pristine flowers wound their way up lithe trunks of rainbow sycamore and silver birch. The perfumed aroma swirled up and around, embracing every organism in its comfort. The relaxing music of running water flowed around me and I found myself wishing I could stay here, immersed in beauty and peace.

A flutter of wings broke the throbbing stillness. Two fencing hummingbirds soared out of the foliage, their beaks clicking together as they parried. Another twitch of the branches revealed the secretive midnight feathers of a black cockatoo, eyeing the fighting birds with disdain.

"Ouch!" the young girl cried.

She batted her small hand at the retreating spines of a green iguana as it rippled along the floor. The small dinosaur fleeing with glee at having defended its territory, a flap of dark fabric clamped in its jaws.

As I watched only a fraction of the life in that room interacting, a change occurred in the young girl. She was listening to something from outside the small haven, her body alert and tense. She wiped the sweat from her ashen face and glanced nervously toward an archway wound with passion fruit. The purple flowers lay open and welcoming. Beyond the archway a door opened. She immediately dropped her gaze to the floor and skirted the room, fleeing through the door before it had a chance to close and block her escape.

Amura was still standing in the middle of the room with a look of serene contentment on her face. She was absorbed in the scene. Maybe like me, she was unable to tell the memory from reality. Or perhaps she just wanted to live it one more time.

"Such a waste of space," the intruder spat with a shake of her head. She shared an unmistakable resemblance to Amura with dark eyes and pale skin, but she had a cruel set to her wan lips. "The only benefit I can see, would be to lure humans in with this stifling display of nature. Their dull minds would enjoy something like this."

The sweat pattered down my back as the humidity pressed in. The perfumed scent of flowers was becoming nauseating, and I shifted uncomfortably. As my back pressed against the wall, a coolness spread through me. The walls were constructed of plain, hard stone. Looking closely, the floor was not made up solely of manicured vegetation but of a rough flagstone. There were no windows to be seen, giving me the feeling of being trapped within a biodome.

A long dragonfly, as blue as a sapphire, buzzed past and was snatched out of the air by a dirty green tree frog. A smacking sound bubbled out as its moist lips snapped shut around its prey.

"Have you decided which way you are going to vote, Amura?"

"Not yet, Karenna."

"We are close to the unity. We need this. You know we are dying without fresh supply."

Amura was not looking at the speaker. She was absorbed in the progress of a golden orb spider, stringing its invisible gallows between two unsuspecting trees.

"You can't keep that servant girl around much longer either. The others think she's just a part of this…" she waved a hand in the air, "like another pet. But there are whispers starting of your pacifism and we can't control it much longer."

"If I do it, it will be for the right reasons," Amura replied, still without looking up.

"You may not remember how it used to be, but I do. The choices…" she trailed off, serpent-like tongue darting out to lick her lips. "Once the other sects are ready, we just need to follow their lead. Once we have access again to the *population*, we can continue as we did. Blame the disappearances on the others. We did it once so we can do it again. History never changes."

The baleful mewing of a bugle filtered into the room.

"Time to make your decision, Princess."

For the first time we were moving. Although I couldn't tell if my body was being pulled forward or if the room was being sucked backward and past me. The cloying humidity was replaced by thin, chilly air. The smell of dust and ancient history replacing the floral scent. As the medley of colors disappeared, a uniform dark stone took its place. Long passageways passed by, barren and drear, winding downward toward an imposing stone door. There were no carvings or personal touches to be seen, just a sheet of barren grey.

A bone-chilling shriek cut through the air as the door was forced open and we entered a huge chamber. Dylan sidled up behind me and whispered in my ear, describing the beings around the room. I crossed my arms tightly over my chest and leaned away from him, but listened despite myself, trying to push my hurt feelings aside long enough to absorb the information.

Once again, the cavernous room had no windows, but it was lit with hundreds of bottled fireflies. The angry vibrations made the light bounce around the room, spinning the shadows in an exhausting dance. There were no chairs, and the beings seemed to have arranged themselves according to seniority.

Amura was along one side with a handful of strange looking creatures. The other wall was lined with around thirty shapeshifters, including the one that had come to her room. They all had a similar look at first glance, but the longer I stared, the more subtle differences showed. The shape of a face, or the arch of an eyebrow, each unique, all terrifying.

Next to Amura someone had begun speaking to the gathered assembly. Dylan whispered 'selkie' in my ear. He looked impossibly human. Tall, lean and handsome. The only difference being a glistening sheen adorning his dark skin like he was immersed in water. His long hair dripped down his back, scraggly and knotted like a centuries old fishing line. He wore no clothes, and I found myself blushing warmly at his beauty.

"We have waited long enough," his voice barked, like a seal. "Our people are ready to embrace the unity, and we are willing to abide by the rules of sustainability."

Dylan noticed my eyes lingering on the speaker and my pink cheeks. He breathed, "They eat human flesh." I raised my shoulder in defense as his hot breath blew unwelcome in my ear.

"We too are ready." Amura's voice rang out, clear and beautiful around the cold room.

There was a murmur of assent from the watchers.

"What about the river dwellers?" The selkie barked again.

An ugly, frog-like creature became the focus. It stood on its bandy back legs, short arms trembling, and suckered fingers pressed together. It bowed low on being addressed.

"Kappa," came the whisper from behind, undeterred by my defensive body language. "It's just the envoy, though, bringing the Kawatora's message."

The Kappa's deep croak echoed around the room. "Rrrready."

The selkie nodded and another two creatures added their assent.

He addressed the crowd again, his mahogany eyes lingering on each soulless black one facing him.

"As you know, friends, fellow members of the Undead, it is your turn for the experiment. We are asking for five volunteers. This year we only ask for those of you that have the self-control *not* to immediately decapitate your human. If your team loses then by all means finish them off, do what you were made to do, but remember the eyes of the Human Government will be watching us closely this year. They think we are the weak link. The one that provides the most danger to them. Of course, as usual they are wrong."

There was a murmur of agreement around the room.

"It's ah maaagic folk, worrrst," croaked the Kappa.

Another acknowledgement from the onlookers, louder this time. The wind which had been still until now, gusted around us as Pixie's eyes flashed.

"We need a success this year. Otherwise, our only option left is war!" The muscles on the selkie's chest rippled as he opened his arms wide, fists clenched.

Amura spoke above the tumult of voices that were swelling in the room. As soon as she raised her translucent hand, they fell quiet. "I know most of you have not been able to feed for decades. I know you are starving. I know you are hurting. As it has been said, we ask only four of you who believe you are strong enough to resist to volunteer and join me."

An uncomfortable silence siphoned the air from the room.

The shapeshifter with the cruel mouth stepped forward. "You cannot volunteer, Princess. We have others willing to go. You are needed here. To keep the peace or to stir up the revolution, whichever is needed."

"Do not argue with me, Karenna." The authority was clear in Amura's voice as the other stepped back into the crowd. "I am going. It is my duty. I will set an example. Then when I win, I will lead the negotiations to bring back our resources to the undead population."

"Princess, with respect," the black-haired shapeshifter from the blue team had now stepped forward, the grisly image of the early-morning blackbird flashed into my mind. "You do not know anything of the outside world. There are many more experienced shifters that can go."

"Like you? Toshin?"

His head cocked to the side, a gleam in his beady eye. "Yes, I'll go, Princess."

I hadn't seen the cylinder filling. I had been too absorbed in the memory. There was no warning crack or breaking of glass. The red stars suddenly exploded from behind, filling the room like grains of sand in an hourglass.

Only one memory left.

NK BROWN

Chapter Twenty-Nine

The same office from Chris's memory appeared around us again. The view from the large windows still showed rolling moorland beyond, but there were a few changes to the inside. The walls were a dated yellow, a threadbare carpet having replaced the polished floors. The central desk was made from an antique-looking rosewood, a stack of untidy papers piled high on one corner. Seated on a leather-bound chair behind it was a middle-aged man. He appeared lost in thought, his finger idly twirling a long moustache, the kind that wouldn't have been out of place a century ago.

There was a hurried knock at the door, and it swung open before the man could speak. A disheveled young man, barely older than me, darted inside and shut the door. His wide eyes scanned the room quickly before he darted over to the desk and perched on the edge of one of the two empty chairs in front. He looked around the room again as sweat slid down his pale face.

"Dad, what's happening?" he said, his voice a loud whisper. "I need to know. I can't keep waiting in the dark. What if he speaks? What if they come for me?"

"Quiet," the man ordered. "And sit still, will you? It's distracting."

The young man jiggled around in his seat, most of his weight being taken by his feet as the chair sat uselessly underneath him.

"I am working on containing the situation. You need to do your part and act normally. We can't have this scandal affecting your sister. She'll have this office one day and something like this would ruin her chances of making governor." His eyes roamed to a photograph framed on his desk. He sat up straighter, puffing out his chest. "The werewolf called Johannes has already been blamed for the murder. The press is going wild, and the Human Government is going to use this as the catalyst for the separation. It will keep all speculation off you, if you control yourself."

"But I can't bear seeing her face everywhere!" He rose, hands clutching at the desk as he leaned toward his father.

"Well, you are going to have to get used to it." There was no warmth in his tone, no sympathy. His voice didn't even change in pitch as he stared at his son. "Now sit down and listen."

The boy resumed his perch at the edge of the chair. His sweaty hands slid over his pockets before digging into his thighs.

"He is due to be executed in two days. I have started an emergency motion to close the portal to the Chasm. It was going to happen anyway once the separation officially started. I have proposed it as a way to stop the other beings from using the spirits for espionage purposes. But it will actually stop the werewolf from coming back in a different form and revealing the truth to anyone who will listen. There are still humans out there with the ability to communicate with the dead and we can't risk him finding one."

"But what if the portal opens again?"

"The government can think of a long-term solution. Maybe some form of experiment or trial when the other beings undoubtably put pressure on us to unite again."

He waved his hand as if dismissing the notion.

"And what about her father?" His voice broke as he leaned toward the desk again.

"He is a human. He will believe what we tell him. Why would he, or anyone else ever doubt that it wasn't the vicious werewolf from next door?"

The young man's hand left his thigh and hovered over his pocket before returning to squeezing his leg again. His knuckles blanched and the tendons of his hand stood up vividly against the bulging blue veins.

This time the father noticed. He narrowed his eyes. "What else have you done?"

A shaking hand dipped into the pocket and a silver heart-shaped locket was produced. The father leaned forward and snatched it from him, throwing it quickly into his desk drawer. The click of the lock snapped through the quiet room. As the father dropped the key into his waistcoat pocket, his eyes darted to the door.

"Where the hell did you get that?" he asked in a hissed whisper, a muscle now twitching in his cheek.

"I had to see her again!" the young man protested. His head fell forward, and he raked his fingers through the untidy blonde hair. "It's all I have left of her."

"You visited the—" he cut himself off with a deep inhale, eyes still blazing. He sat up straighter in his chair. "I'll deal with it."

The cord tightened around my waist and the jerk pulled me violently into the present.

NK BROWN

Chapter Thirty

As the now familiar red mist cleared, I found myself standing in an uncomfortable circle. We had all been positioned by an unseen hand like soldiers on a battlefield.

Chris stood with one hand nervously stroking the handle of his annihilator. He was pale, and the pulse pounded in his throat. Amura was directly opposite him. Her eyes were fixed on his face. Her teeth were bared and there was a ferocity emanating from her that no human being could ever possess.

Opposite me, Dylan hovered. His feet barely touched the ground, every inch of his body thrust forward, ready to spring toward me. His eyes were wide and there was a slight pucker above his eyebrows as the anticipation froze him in place. I knew that my lips were pursed, that my eyes were hard and unforgiving, and I didn't care. He deflated slowly across from me, and a small twinge gently kneaded my stomach. I ignored it.

Pixie was sandwiched between Dylan and Amura. It was disconcerting to see her so far from Chris's side. She had shadowed him like Dylan had me. She looked exposed, almost fragile. She was out of her element.

We were at the edge of a thick forest. The safety and comfort of the solid boughs whispered to me to join their ranks. I wanted nothing more than to hide amongst their leaves and avoid this showdown. On the other side was a smooth, manmade surface. The compacted floor was dull and clean, reeking of oil and tar. It was completely exposed. The only object being a blood-red raised dais in the center.

The trees hovered around the edges of the circular crater like spectators in an arena, drawing focus toward the lid of the boxcar platform. A small rectangular strip of paper fluttered gently on its surface. It was held in place by a quill, speared by the nib, its colored feathers standing proudly like the fletching of an arrow.

No one moved.

Everyone was frozen by their private thoughts. I glanced back over at the paper and taking a deep breath, cautiously crept toward it. Even Dylan did not follow me. Nothing moved and no sound came from the dais. There was just an eerie stillness hanging in the air.

I eased the quill out of the paper and scanned the note. The words were elegantly written in a beautiful cursive and as my brain absorbed them, my body started to panic.

I turned back toward the others. It was too late to pretend I hadn't read it. I knew the blood had drained from my face despite the frantic pumping of my heart. Focusing on the immaculately smooth floor, I retraced my steps out of the circle, the note somehow now scrunched up in my balled fist.

Resuming my previous position, I cleared my throat. "Congratulations, red team, on progressing to zone one. Your teamwork and ability to resolve conflict has so far been remarkable. We hope you now have a greater understanding of each other after sharing your histories and can unite for the final problem." My throat was so dry, the words scratched it raw as I choked them out. "You have one hour to decide which human deserves to complete the experiment with you and dispose of the other."

The message hung heavy in the silence.

****

One hour to end the experiment.

There was an explosion of energy. In the blink of an eye, Pixie threw herself at me. Her eyes flashed black, and her sharpened nails drove toward me.

A vicious growl erupted. The auburn fur of the werewolf slammed into her, knocking her sideways. He flattened himself down in front of me, creating an impenetrable barrier, his furious snarling filling the air.

Pixie composed herself and began brushing invisible material away from her clothes. She stood facing Dylan, a look of contempt on her face. Chris's surprised form was visible behind her, eyebrows raised but eyes hard.

"I was not attacking her, you idiot half-blood," she blustered, not yet in control. "I just wanted to read the note." Her eyes slowly regained their ever-changing shades of purple and the serene look painted itself back on her face. "Can I see it girl, yes?"

I held it out behind Dylan with trembling fingers. An intrusive gust of wind snatched it and carried it over to her. She read it over twice and then handed it behind her to Chris. He didn't even glance at the words. He ripped it up and threw it onto the ground at his feet.

"*We* need to discuss this calmly as a group, no?"

She fixed her eyes on Dylan, as if he were the one who had tried to kill me. He grudgingly straightened, the bristling fur being replaced by smooth, olive skin. The snarling died away, but he didn't move from in front of me. The muscles of his back strained through his shirt and his fingers twitched. His hands repeatedly balled into fists and then unclenched as he waited.

Anna, leave now. Don't play their game.

"The message is clear. There is no loophole here. I also know that, although not a popular choice, there is only one that is correct, no?"

Dylan cocked his head slightly. I knew he was narrowing his eyes and clenching his jaw.

"We all want the same thing. That is our strength

as a group. It was plain to see in the memories. We want a unified government. We want freedom to mix with each other. To fall in love with whomever our hearts want, irrespective of the species. To do that we need to make a sacrifice." She paused to let the words sink in.

Don't trust the Human Government—they have been thwarting the experiment from the start. They don't want the unity.

I didn't know if the spirit's message was tainted due to the memory we had just seen or if the warning was genuine. They could have chosen not to participate once their role in the Chasm was complete, yet they were still here. Still communicating with me.

"We need to be in a position of power within the government, to make sure our voices are heard. There is only one choice, yes?"

Dylan growled in answer.

Pixie continued, her voice taking on a persuasive note that seeped into our ears like honey. Amura waited in her original place, her expression now blank. I willed her to say something, to be the voice of reason. Hoped she would be on my side if it came to that. Her black eyes flashed to me briefly. They held no malice, but they held no warmth. She gave an almost imperceptible shake of her head and leapt into the air. The lean form of a red-tailed hawk appeared. The white stripe of feathers on her tail waving like a flag of peace as she flew up into the nearest pine tree.

My heart sank as reluctantly I turned my gaze back to the figures in front. Chris had not moved, but his hand still caressed the handle of his weapon. Would he use it on me? I almost looked at him like a brother now. As irritating as he was, the advice he'd given had always been meant well. It was based on a wealth of experience that I had not yet discovered for myself. In truth, he would do a better job in government than I would.

"Chris," I said, "I think you should take the backpack. The Vessel of Unity."

Everyone stared at me.

"No, Anna," Dylan growled. "Don't give it to him. Don't give up so easily—"

"I'm not giving up, Dylan," I interrupted. "I've said all along, there is no need to kill anyone. Isn't the whole point of this experiment to show that we can all be peaceful? I think Chris would—"

"Girl, give me the Vessel of Unity, not him." Pixie cut me off. "Chris will already have a position in government. Remember his memory? It is I who would be able to do the best and bring the separated governments together, yes? Without me, none of you would have got this far."

"It was thanks to Anna we all got this far," Dylan snarled at her. "She was the one able to communicate with the spirit. She was the only one of us able to complete the task in the Chasm and even though she's been attacked, burned and traumatized by every being here she is still the one advocating for peace."

Anna, if you won't listen to me then listen to Dylan. Do not trust either of them. Remember, Chris works for the government.

I unhooked the backpack and reached inside. Settled at the bottom of the bag was a delicate silver necklace. I wrapped my fingers around the heart-shaped locket and pulled it out. Pixie and Chris's eyes remained locked on its progress. Dylan growled loudly but made no move to stop me. Dropping the backpack on the ground, I flung the necklace over at Chris. He snatched it out of the air and his sharp brown eyes swiveled to mine.

As the corners of his mouth fell down, I knew what he would do.

NK BROWN

Chapter Thirty-One

Fifty minutes to end the experiment.

Dylan was distracted by Pixie. He was having a hard time keeping himself calm and his voice would erupt suddenly, jarring alongside the eloquent sentences Pixie was constructing. They had returned to arguing over which one of us deserved to die.

"If he has the Vessel of Unity now," Dylan growled, "then he automatically gets a free pass. There is no need to kill Anna. There is the loophole."

The breeze was warm and inviting as it circled around us. It was slowly bringing leaves and twigs from the encircling forest and scattering them around our feet. The smell of pine and earth was soothing, hypnotic even.

"The fate of all the segregated beings relies on us, wolf. We are so close to success, yes? We cannot take even the smallest chance just for the sake of this…"

I saw it before him. Saw the fingers hesitate as they stroked the metal, as if tasting its smooth surface. They silently coiled around it like a python.

A sudden gust of wind blew the debris up and around, blinding me, choking me.

"Run!"

I grabbed Dylan's arm and jerked him to the side as a crackling burst of electricity shot past him. The stink of burned flesh and smoldering cotton barely registered. He let out an anguished howl but ran with me as I dragged him toward the woods. I hadn't been quick enough to stop him from getting hurt, but at least he was alive.

I didn't know where I was going, my feet just flew under me, pounding the earth in blind panic. I let go of Dylan's arm and rubbed my hand across my eyes. The flying earth had lodged under my eyelids. Stinging tears streamed down my face and all around me the woods wobbled as if underwater.

We tore through the undergrowth, brambles snagged on my clothes and ripped deep gashes in my skin. I risked a glance behind but couldn't see anything except the blurred outline of green and brown soldiers, scrutinizing our retreat into unknown territory.

After a few miles he slowed and came to a stop. Pulling up beside him, I dug my hands into my hips, trying my best to wheeze and splutter silently. He was listening intently, head cocked.

It was hard to tell in the moment who Chris had been aiming at. The only way to get to me would likely be by taking Dylan out first. But if he did that then no one would win. What was his end game?

I looked at Dylan again. The burn on his arm made me wince. The angry red flesh gaped wide, with the skin pulling back at the edges. There was a strong smell of roasted meat coming from it and it glistened as the serous fluid pooled over the surface.

"Dylan, we need to—"

He cut me off with a 'shh,' still listening to someone or something my ears couldn't pick up. The air here was still and cool. Not even a gentle breeze stirred around us. All the leaves of the trees stood rigid, as if waiting for instructions. We were not safe. This was where she was most powerful, camouflaged, at home.

He winced and twitched his arm, and I tried again.

"Dylan, your arm, we need—"

He put his hand tightly over my mouth and pushed me back against the wide trunk of an oak tree. The sharp splinters of bark dug into my back as he pressed his body against mine to keep me still.

"Don't you dare bite me this time." His eyes were

serious, but his mouth twitched slightly.

I glared at him. I thought about kicking him, but at this point he was my only ally, so I stayed quiet, watching him curiously. As he listened to the silence his yellow eyes scanned repetitively. Back and forth. Back and forth. He wasn't focused on anything in the foreground, but he could see something out there. I had a flashback to the young girl's head, clutched in his father's large hands in the family photo. How could they even call what they did a sport if there was no competition?

His face relaxed a fraction, and he turned his penetrating gaze on me. Despite my hurt at his betrayal, my breath hitched, and I softened into him. He removed his hand from my mouth and stroked the side of my cheek, my skin flushing at his touch.

"What you saw wasn't real, Anna," he whispered, bringing his face within inches of mine.

As he moved to kiss me, I turned my face to the side, pressing my hands into his chest to move him away.

"Don't lie to me!" I snapped, unable to whisper back. "You've been playing a game this whole time. I know what we saw was true because everyone else's memories were real. Mine was real."

My hands still pushed against him, but he hadn't moved. His body was strong and warm as I stood there trapped.

"I'm not going to let you go unless you listen to me." The stress broke through in his words, transforming them into a throaty growl.

"Is there even any point?" I managed to lower my voice to a hissed whisper. "One or both of us is going to die very soon. We have more important things to think about."

"It's not more important to me."

I stopped short of rolling my eyes and glared at

him again. A few seconds passed until I sighed heavily, which he took as permission to carry on the conversation.

"I'm sorry for what you saw. The glimpse you got of my life. I never made any promises that day. I was forced into the experiment, just as you were. But, unlike you, I never wanted to get out again. I had no intention of returning to that life. What I really wanted was for my younger brothers to see another way of living. One without all the hatred and violence and terror. I knew I would probably have to die to make that come true.

"I wanted to make sure I didn't hurt anyone, but for the right reasons, not because my father had blackmailed me. I had no idea how I was going to do it, how I was supposed to control the urge that had been instilled in me and encouraged for so long. But then I saw you."

His hand tentatively started to caress my face again and his throat quivered as he swallowed. A nervous flush painted his cheeks beneath the stubble.

"I watched you in the clearing at the start for some time. I was far enough away that no one could sense my presence. I felt something that I had never experienced before. I wanted to be close to you, to know you. I needed to protect you, but I didn't know if I could trust myself to do it."

His hand slid down and cupped my chin, tilting my face up to his. His other hand wound around my waist softly, warming my skin. His mouth twitched in a shy smile, and he leaned down and kissed my cheek. My skin tingled from the touch, spreading heat up my body.

His lips moved down to my jaw, my neck, gently caressing. I drew in a shallow breath and lifted my head up higher as he kissed me softly at the delicate hollow of my throat. My hands stopped pushing him away and my fingers wound into the fabric of his shirt drawing him hard against me.

A low growl escaped from his throat as his mouth moved up and met mine. An urgency flowed into his body as we both forgot where we were. Forgot who we were. And lost ourselves in the moment.

A cool breeze filtered through the trees, softly rustling the leaves, warning of its approach. Dylan pulled away and scanned the woods around us. I shivered as his warmth left me allowing the anxiety to gnaw away in my gut again.

"I think it is only the wind this time," he murmured.

"What happens if we don't complete the experiment?" I asked.

He shifted closer to me again, rubbing my arms with his warm hands, the rough palms oddly soothing. "They send something else to finish the job."

It was common knowledge that nobody left the experiment alive unless you were in the winning team. But they never showed what happened. There were many theories, and it was widely accepted that none of them were pleasant. The coverage always cut away to a promotional video of some kind.

I expected that for Dylan and me, a high ranking official somewhere would proclaim that he had attacked and killed me. Then they would show a clip of werewolves attacking humans or some scientific study emphasizing the differences in our DNA that made them monsters incapable of human emotions or self-control. It probably wouldn't even be questioned by either side and then the division between the beings would be strengthened even further.

"Maybe Pixie does have a point," I said.

He glared at me.

"We need to circle back slowly. Figure out what

we are going to do."

He was still looking at me, suspicion covering his face.

Remember the memories. Think about what you heard and did not hear.

"Now is the not the time for riddles. If you have a message, just tell me," I grumbled.

But no answer came.

Chapter Thirty-Two

Thirty-five minutes to end the experiment.

Dylan scanned the shadows of the forest again before setting off quickly. His feet made no noise against the soft earth, the pine needles cushioning every advancing step. I jogged after him, doing my best to keep pace and be quiet.

I knew when I left my small kitchen that I would never return. I also knew from years of propaganda and failed experiments that the union was never going to happen if the same steps were repeated over and over. There had to be a change.

I knew what I was going to do.

We stopped a half mile from the clearing. The breeze was still mild, and I hardly felt it as the adrenaline pulsed through my body.

"Do you want me to take the annihilator?" Dylan whispered. "Are you going to be able to kill him?"

"I'll keep it."

He studied my face, unable to read my expression. "What do you think of me?" he asked.

I mumbled something incoherent, aware of the intensity in his face and the hunger in his eyes. The honey irises glowed, silky and smooth, and my stomach fluttered.

"Am I enough for you?" he whispered.

"Why wouldn't you be?"

The corner of his mouth twitched before breaking into a wide grin. "Good. I don't know how to read human emotions. You're like an indecipherable language."

I snorted. "I'm literally the same as you. Except I cannot change into a werewolf whenever I want."

His gaze left my face, his attention returning to

the clearing, eyes darting between the dense trees, penetrating the gaps before connecting with mine again.

"I'd do all this again, you know, whatever the outcome, if it meant meeting you."

The heat stampeded into my cheeks. "Me too," I said. And it was true.

"I'll find you again," he said, "when this is over. Wherever we end up."

I swallowed and nodded.

I think she killed him.

"Who killed who?" I asked, jolting back into the present.

Dylan looked at me puzzled.

I can only sense two beings in the distance, both not human.

"Why would she do that? He was her pawn. She needed him."

Maybe she thought it was the only way to win.

"What is it?" Dylan asked. His hand gripped the bark of the nearest tree. Small shards of fawn mulch fluttered to the floor like the letter his father had torn up in his kitchen.

I filled Dylan in on the conversation.

"Then let's find out," he growled.

He kissed me gently and took my hand, leading me carefully through the ranks of pine and oak. The smell of oil became stronger, as the man-made circle of destruction carved into the defenseless woods approached in front of us. I took out the annihilator from my jeans and grasped the now cool metal.

One pulse left. One shot to make a difference.

****

Twenty minutes to end the experiment.

"This is as far as my father got, you know."

He didn't answer but he was listening intently.

"They didn't broadcast it, but the official announcement said there was a disagreement with the centaur on the team."

He nodded slightly. The news was unsurprising to him.

"What are the chances that two people from the same family are picked?"

He shrugged and made a motion with his hand for me to be quiet.

Not high.

I nodded.

"How far can you see?" I asked Dylan.

"Further than you," came the growl.

I rolled my eyes and stood quietly, hands on hips whilst I waited.

"I can see where she is waiting," he whispered. "No sign of Chris and none of Amura either."

"It just doesn't seem right though, does it?" A prickling unease crept across my skin, raising the hairs on my arms.

"Well, the spirit couldn't see him either and you trust them, don't you?"

"Well, yes."

"Then let's go, we're running out of time. Let's get this over with."

I sighed loudly. Every instinct I owned screamed at me not to go. But Dylan had started stalking through the trees, blending with the long shadows. The pine needles absorbed the sound of his approach, hidden even from the wind.

I followed at a distance, unable to move as quietly and a lot less confident in the outcome than he was. Something was different with the scene. Barely ten yards away was the opening in the trees, where the black tarmac stretched out widely. It looked smaller than before. Or maybe the surrounding trees were taller. Had I not been paying attention?

I crept forward until there was only a thin line of shrubs hiding my approach. Pixie was standing at the edge of the semi-circular crater and Dylan was almost in front of her now. It took a second, then an alarm blared loudly in my mind. *Semi-circle.*

I began to scream a warning, for Dylan to get out, but the wind drowned the sound of my voice. The tallest trees crowding the crater melted away. They drooped and sagged, morphed into leaves, sticks and debris that piled up around the floor.

In the center of them, barely a foot away from Dylan, were the sharp brown eyes and downward smile that I should never have trusted. Chris held the annihilator in one hand, aimed square at Dylan's chest. In the other, the silver necklace was twined around his fingers, his knuckles white.

A tittering laugh blew over to me. "Haven't you heard the saying, girl? It's just the wind playing tricks on you." The cold air knifed through me as I stood there helplessly. "Now, out you come, yes?"

Chapter Thirty-Three

Ten minutes to end the experiment.

It was a stalemate. They thought it was a checkmate. The square barrel was barely a foot away from Dylan's heaving chest. It held steady. No wavering. No indecision. It only had one job to do, and it knew it well. Take out the pawn and kill the king.

Pixie was standing a few feet away, swaying slightly as a warm breeze rustled her clothes and caused her hair to proudly cascade down her shoulders like armor on a knight. Her purple eyes gleamed and a cruel smile lit her face. "There is only one choice, girl." The wind blew gently, with an air of superiority. It knew nothing could stop it now. "You want him to live, yes?"

I nodded.

There was an almost imperceptible movement from the low branch of the tall oak tree behind them. A small dark spider with a flash of color on its leathery back floated gently downward. An invisible thread of gossamer silk acted like a guide rope as the breeze unwittingly steered it toward the target. It landed on the crinkled edge of Chris's collar, unbeknown to all other eyes.

"Then make the sacrifice, girl."

****

One minute to end the experiment.

Dylan gave a muffled whine, the sound carried away from my ears by the wind's manipulative breath. My arm hung limply by my side, waiting for instructions. I raised the weapon that was still clutched in my hand. You can't hide from the elements. You can't deceive a being that can plunge into the most secretive corners of your mind.

I accepted my fate and twisted my wrist around, so I was looking straight down the inky barrel. My hands were slick on the handle and my heart thrashed loudly in my chest. I was ready for this to be over. There was only one right choice to make.

Digging my finger into the narrow strip of metal, I pulled the trigger.

Chapter Thirty-Four

The crackle of electricity thrust past my face, the powerful heat smacking my head back. Directly behind me the brick-red lid of the boxcar exploded. The smell of charred metal and burning oil enveloped us in a moment of absolute stillness.

Then chaos descended.

The tiny black widow spider reared silently up on her back legs and plunged downward, sinking her deadly fangs into the throbbing pulse of the neck below her. Chris screamed, eyes wide with horror, clutching at his neck as the weapon dropped from his hands.

At the same time Pixie launched herself toward me, eyes black pools of fury. Her sharpened nails stretched like talons shooting toward my face. She was knocked off course as a rush of auburn fur collided with her, snarling and growling. He pinned her to the floor and gnashed his teeth against her neck. But she was too quick and melted out from underneath him as he bit into the raging wind.

The spider on Chris's neck was growing. Its red bull's eye stretched and engorged as the blood flowed into the greedy body like a tick on a mouse. As it grew to the size of his fist, he fought with it, trying to tear it from his jugular. The fangs ripped free, tearing a long gash down the fragile blue vein—strong iron-rich blood oozed and spilled down his torso. He wobbled unsteadily, face frozen in a confused look of terror and disbelief.

Pixie's lithe form distorted into a monstrous hunched figure. It had no face and showed no mercy as she lashed out across Dylan's back. Angry red slashes appeared as if the wind held invisible knives in its cold fingers. He howled with pain, the sound piercing straight to my core.

Dylan writhed and snarled on the ground, flattened by the inhuman presence hanging over him. Unable to stop myself I rushed toward him, but after a few steps my feet suddenly froze. It was like someone had taken control of the wheel and I was forced to ride as a passenger. I strained and pushed and urged my limbs to move, but they stood resolutely still.

Anna, you need to run, not fight.

Chris clutched unsuccessfully at his neck, his face deathly pale. The slender figure of Amura stretched out of the huge spider, blood dripping from her mouth. Her long fingers twitched at her sides and then she leapt behind him. She met my wide eyes with a satisfied smile—the look of revenge. She gripped him tightly and tore his head from his shoulders. As his body hit the ground, she was on him once again. The bile flew into my mouth as the sounds of ripping and tearing assaulted my ears.

Go and find your father.

Dylan managed to drag himself to his feet and lunged toward Pixie's monstrous figure again. The wind knocked him back with such force his head hit the tarmac with a sickening smack. He was momentarily stunned, and the wind howled with pleasure.

"Dylan!" I screamed.

My feet were still stuck, my body immobile. I strained against the invisible chains holding me fast.

You need to run. Now.

"I can't leave him to die!"

He will find you.

Amura tore herself away from the shredded mound of flesh in front of her and leapt onto the twisted figure hovering above the werewolf. She encircled her tightly, leaving no space for the wind to slide its cold fingers in and prize her free. Dylan struggled to his feet. The rage burned in his eyes, his mouth stretched wide in a furious snarl. Blood poured from the gashes on his back and his auburn fur was plastered to his face with sweat, saliva, and blood.

The distant whirring of an engine seeped into my consciousness. The ominous rhythm was like the pounding of a tribal drum, announcing the end of the game and the beginning of the massacre.

Dylan snapped and slashed at the figure. Even though it was being held tightly by Amura, he kept contacting only the thin air. The clashing of his jaws biting together added to the noise.

Suddenly the engine was directly above the clearing, a large shadow blocking out the light. The whirring blades swirled the leaves and debris creating a cloud of thick dust that enveloped us all.

"Dylan! Amura! We need to go now!"

Amura's arms relaxed and she sprang away from the spinning shape, but Dylan wouldn't leave. A large net descended from the belly of the plane. As it touched the floor, a crackle of electricity thrummed through it, rendering all magic useless. Dylan's human form returned, closely followed by the shimmering hair of Pixie. He grabbed at the net, his fingers slipping through the holes before being jerked backward by a flash of lightning. He lay on his back panting whilst Pixie watched with one eyebrow raised and arms folded.

Amura sped past me. Not confined to the rules of the experiment, she transitioned into a cheetah and raced off through the woods. The only thing visible was the black tip of her tail, swinging from side to side like the point of a compass as she weaved through the trees.

I'll get him out.

The air around me shimmered. A torpedo of

energy shot out and exploded on contact with the net. A jagged hole appeared, and Dylan scrambled to his feet and forced himself through. The net snapped and crackled, singing his skin as he escaped.

Run!

This time I listened. I turned and ran into the woods.

Chapter Thirty-Five

Dylan was instantly beside me, pushing me forward and away from the plane. I glanced back as we ran to see Pixie standing there calmly. She wasn't even trying to escape. A ray of light reflected from the silver object hanging around her neck. She gave me a smug smile as I wrenched my head back around.

"The spirit, Dylan?" I panted.

He didn't slow. He didn't even look back. "They will be taken," he said. His hand closed around my arm, dragging me forward faster. "I could feel the spirit block the hole in the net after I pushed myself through, stopping *her* from escaping." His fingers ratcheted tighter, possibly because he knew what I would be trying to do next. "The spirit will be sent back to the Chasm."

My heart throbbed at the idea of their capture. Of being trapped back in Purgatory with no hope of escape. After everything they had done guiding us through this experiment.

"We need to go back and—"

"Don't be stupid. They are after us already. Can't you hear the footsteps?"

"Of course I can't hear people's footsteps over all this noise!"

If I escaped, I would do everything I could to make it back to the Chasm and release them.

"Not people. The security teams. Dozens of them." He glanced at me. "We need to split up. They will go after me as I will be harder to find."

"We can't split up. Neither of us knows where we are going and we're going to be better—"

"Just listen to me for once!" he growled. "I know how to hunt. I know what they'll try to do and—"

"I'm not leaving you, so just—"

He slid to a stop, dragging me with him and lowered his face to mine.

"Please," he whispered.

I looked into his eyes and my stomach churned.

A beat passed.

I nodded.

"Go straight. Don't look back. I'll find you again."

He pulled me toward him and kissed me hard. Before I could draw a breath, he backed away and sped off in the other direction. The loud cry of the werewolf reverberated around the forest.

The approaching whine of the engine startled me back to life. The trees around began to sway, dust swirling up and into the gusting wind.

I tore through the woods, lungs screaming and legs burning. The panic was overriding the guilt at leaving Dylan behind, but it was a fine line. My body was on the verge of collapse, but the terror at being caught was stronger. I had no idea where I was going but I had to get as far from the sound of the plane as possible.

We had failed. We had done what so many teams had done before us, turned on each other, and left a wealth of destruction in our wake. What was worse, was the knowledge that the experiment would run again. The same cycle. The same deaths. A never-ending wormhole of propaganda from the governments.

As I ran, the whining of the engine became fainter. It crashed down through the trees toward the clearing. I could vividly imagine the armed guards swarming out like locusts, destroying all living creatures in their paths. Would they capture Dylan? Amura?

Slowing to a jog, the trees around me thinned and the earth softened. I splashed through a muddy channel in the ground, the fresh, salty scent of the ocean washing over me. I could hear the crashing waves now, but they were still far in the distance. Only a soft lapping filtered through.

A wide river opened before me, and I slowed to a walk. The banks were slippery and sticky but the current looked slow, gently ushering fallen leaves along the midnight surface and into the distance. I slid down and toward the water. If I travelled through it for long enough, the tracking guards may not be able to follow my scent. But, then neither would Dylan.

Gingerly I tested my footing in the current and waded across. The water rose quickly to my waist but went no further. It was cool and welcome, and I wished it could wash away all the nightmares as it would the dirt. Not far up ahead was a depression in the opposite bank. It was a perfect triangle and stood out against the thick, brown mud.

As I neared it, a small boat appeared. I hadn't noticed it from afar as it was perfectly camouflaged. The bow was a muddy brown, and the body was the soft greens and blues of the swirling water. It must be enchanted. But it could be a trap. There were no other options—I had to get out, I needed to disappear. As if to spur my decision, the rumble of the engine crept toward me again in the still air. I dragged the boat off the bank and climbed in.

I slumped on the floor watching my legs vanish, replaced instead with the exact hues of the swirling water below. There were no oars or anything with which to steer so I just lay down and drifted with the current toward the open ocean. Rocking back and forth like a newborn baby, the motion soothing me into an exhausted sleep.

****

My ears awoke first, the sound of the soft lapping of white-tipped waves against a solid object stirred me. Then the strong, fresh smell of salt water filled my nostrils, itching but refreshing. I blinked awake and found myself gazing into the captivating sea-green eyes of a stranger. The boat gently tipped from side to side, but the eyes held steady.

As I focused, a golden trident appeared, gripped in his strong hand. He leaned back from my face giving a nod of approval, the gesture graceful and in harmony with the swells beneath and dipped the trident into the deep blue water. He spun it slightly, the movement like the manipulation of a tiller and the boat obeyed, angling itself to align with the sea breeze and our momentum increased.

"We have another pick up to make, Grey," he said.

His voice was rich and beautiful, and I found myself openly staring at him. I had no idea whether he was talking to me or the boat. I struggled up into a sitting position and hoisted myself onto one of the narrow wooden benches.

The ocean stretched unbroken for miles in every direction. The sky was lit with soft pastels of pinks and oranges as sunrise began. There was a break in the surf around the bow and I leaned forward as a silvery shape floated upward. It broke the surface of the water, its silver streamlined fur sparkling as sunlight refracted from water droplets pouring off its body. A seal sliced through the air and plunged back into the water.

I gasped, unable to stop myself as the animal's joy ran through me. The seal leapt again, this time twisting its body like a corkscrew, entering the water perfectly as it completed its maneuver. It swam alongside the boat and then glided on the surface. Its long whiskers, full of expression and emotion twitched and fumbled in the air, before the red eyes gave me a nod of approval and disappeared beneath the waves. Disappointed, I watched the choppy water swallow its form. But I also had a moment of recognition, I had seen those eyes before. My foggy brain being unable to remember where or when.

The trident was being eased slowly out of the water. In response, the forward motion of the boat ceased, and we bobbed like a cork. A foreign sound rose above the gentle tapping of the waves against the boat. It was a frantic, uncontrolled noise and I couldn't find the cause.

A shape jerked toward us. The front arms splashing noisily, slapping at the water, the back legs kicking frantically. The damp auburn hair and familiar stubble lining the face of a being completely out of its element in the majestic ocean.

My heart swelled and I threw my arms into the air and waved manically. Dylan reached the boat, and the strong hand of the merman tightened around his arm and hauled him in. I threw my arms around him and buried my face in his neck. Inhaling deeply, I let the smell of cinnamon wash over me, not caring about the freezing water soaking into my clothes.

He gave a throaty growl, and I pulled my face back to look at him. But he gripped my head and forced me toward him again, his lips hard and urgent against mine. His other hand dug into my waist, gripping too tightly. On instinct, I tried to move away, to protect myself, but he held firm.

The pressure vanished as he was thrown backward into the stern of the boat.

"That is not how you treat a human, Red," the merman admonished. "You need to be gentle. They are delicate. They are fragile."

The sea-green eyes turned back to me again and

he ran a long, wet finger softly down my arm. A chill spread across my skin at his touch, closely followed by warmth rushing my body. His eyes were enchanting me, pulling me to him, but I offered no resistance. The rest of his words were lost, as they rushed past me like running water.

His hand was still trailing down my arm, no hint of danger in his calm voice. "Their skin tears so easily. One wrong move and they can be ripped apart."

Dylan snarled, his eyes focused on the merman's hand as he continued to trace invisible lines on my skin. The sound brought me to my senses just in time as a line of bristling red fur rippled up his back. His muscles bulged and contorted before he launched himself toward us.

I scrambled up and dove off the boat and into the cold ocean. I swam about twenty yards before looking back, treading water amongst the calm waves. Dylan was trying to control himself. He was caught mid-transformation, his shape grotesquely distorted, not man and not beast. He whined softly, the sound carried back to me over the light sea breeze. The adrenaline rushed from my body, replaced by pity. But most strongly by guilt, as I had abandoned him again.

I swam cautiously back to the small boat and around to the side furthest from him. Gripping the slick sides, I kicked hard, pulling myself out of the water. I dropped down heavily onto the floor with a wet splashing sound, the weight of my water-logged clothes heavier than expected.

His honey eyes were wide and full of anguish. Remaining in the relative safety of the far corner, ready to dive back into the water if he came at me again, I softly spoke. "Dylan, it's okay. You didn't hurt me. You can change back now."

His eyes remained locked on mine as his contorted muscles smoothed. The fur covering half of his body receded and his mouth closed, wiping the grimace from his face.

The trident reappeared in the water next to me, the sea-green eyes watching from under the water. The merman broke the surface and effortlessly vaulted into the boat, resuming his position at the stern seated next to me. The boat began to glide through the waves again.

None of us spoke.

Dylan remained awkwardly poised at the far end, and I watched him uncertainly. Then I noticed red straps digging into his broad shoulders.

"Do you have the backpack, Dylan?"

He glanced down in surprise and, nodding, removed it and tossed it gently toward me. I opened it quickly and greedily drank from the red canteen. The water was stale and there was salt stuck to the rim from its ordeal in the waves, but I didn't care. My stomach protested loudly at being forgotten and I remembered the dried food.

I walked unsteadily toward him, one hand gripping the bag and the other clutching at the side of the rocking boat for support and gingerly sat next to him. He shifted his body away from me, so we weren't touching, but accepted one of the high calorie bars I offered. The movement of the boat brought our arms together and then forced us apart again as we rode the swell.

The silence deepened as we glided across the waves as uncomfortable as strangers.

NK BROWN

Chapter Thirty-Six

We continued across the open sea, the small boat as much a part of the waves as the frolicking seal had been. There was no land in sight, just an empty expanse of blue sky stretching to meet the horizon. Dylan had been silent for a while, thinking things through in the privacy of his own mind.

Eventually he spoke, his voice a controlled whisper. "Have I hurt you?"

I didn't know whether it was better to lie and save him from the emotional pain or to tell the truth and spare myself from future physical pain. So, I compromised. "Sometimes."

He didn't seem to like that response and lapsed back into a moody silence.

"What happened back in the woods?" I asked. "After I ran." Then as a pang of guilt punched me hard in the stomach, I added, "I'm sorry for leaving you out there."

His eyes were soft as they turned to me, and a rueful smile tugged at his lips. "I'm glad you finally listened to me. We all did it for you, you know."

He took a deep breath, forcing his mind and soul back in time to the woods. He told the story in his own way. Skipping ahead and then going back. As a listener it felt very unnatural, but he lived through emotions, and it made sense to him.

"I knew that they were gaining on us. I could hear from the snarls that they were half-werewolves the government was using. We used to laugh about them back at home. They were inferior to us in every way. The humans chose them because they thought they carried all the attributes we have, just without our temperament. But we could run rings around them any day. There were a few pulses fired, as the security guards realized their inadequacy, but none came close to me." He grinned.

Clearing his throat, he continued in a whisper. "The plane seemed to hover over the area for a while. I knew it wouldn't see me. I was too quick and adept at hiding myself in the woods, having practiced over the years, hunting and outsmarting humans. They had wasted a lot of time pursuing me in circles and I hoped that it had given you enough time to get far away. I didn't hear it land again so it probably left the guards out their searching. I suspect they will come back armed with better scavengers, those more accustomed to finding the escaped subjects from the experiment.

"I lost your scent at the river. I hoped you would have purposely gone in to cover your tracks as I couldn't smell you again on the other side. You would have been getting tired and would have been stupid to have gone upriver, so I ran alongside the water to the sea. I stayed in the werewolf form as recognizing your scent amongst so many other distractions was now part of my DNA. I could go on autopilot and let the beast in me hunt you down."

I shivered at the terminology. He didn't move to put an arm around me like he would have done previously, and my body slumped a little.

"On reaching the open ocean, I still didn't have your scent again. You must have gone out to sea, but even my powerful eyes could not see through the magic of this boat. Not knowing which way to go for sure, I set off toward the East. Something just seemed to pull me in that direction. I followed the coast for miles, scanning the waves. Eventually I spotted *him*," he tipped his head disdainfully toward the merman, "and he motioned for me to swim out."

"Do you know where Amura went?" I asked.

He shook his head.

The merman supplied the answer. "She's going on ahead. She did not need to be collected on route."

Neither of them added any more. Dylan resumed his sullen silence at the merman's interruption of his story and the merman resumed his focus back out to sea. I searched the clear skies for Amura, expecting to see those black eyes staring down at me from the body of an albatross or some other exotic sea bird that I couldn't name. But the sky was disappointingly clear.

The loss of the spirit weighed heavy on my heart, but I felt nothing toward the capture of Pixie. My brain had completely forgotten all about Chris as well during the trauma and his downward smile floated back into my mind.

The familiar ache of loss like the pangs of an empty stomach, filtered through my core as once again those closest to me had been torn apart.

NK BROWN

Chapter Thirty-Seven

Time soared by and the sun began to dip low in the sky, the weak rays tired after a long day.

A small spit of land was approaching. Behind the narrow, sandy beach lay tall, jagged cliffs. Their faces were as white as the crests of the waves that pummeled and shaped them. The tide was out, and the sea calm so the merman steered the boat gently into the shallow water and beached on the crumbling golden sand.

"Where are we going?" I probably should have asked the question sooner.

"We have another day of travel before us," answered the merman.

"That's not helpful," Dylan grumbled.

The merman considered this, his beautiful eyes staring unfocused across the darkening ocean. Then he focused back on my face, his mouth curving into a serene smile. My stomach twisted as once again the pull of attraction grasped at me and I did nothing to stop it.

There were many legends surrounding the merpeople. They were gentle and kind, but darkness lay within. Humans were often snagged in their nets, lured in by their charm. What those that were caught experienced never fully emerged, but they told strange tales of underwater worlds and adoration. However, those of shrewd mind noticed that the stories were always told with a glazed expression, a faraway look on their faces. The words they spoke were dreamlike and unrealistic.

The legends that I knew alluded to the trickery. The magic that covers up the deceit and the truth about what really happened to those that crossed their path. I knew all of this and believed the dark tales. And yet, I offered no resistance to the allure of his sea-green gaze.

"There are many of us," continued the merman, "that have decided to stop waiting on the results of the experiment to allow a unity. No progress has been made over many years and countless lives lost in the process. We have an outcrop of beings, that includes high ranking representatives from almost all the major governments. The only ones missing are of course the humans, as they are the ones stalling the process and now, because of the end to this most recent experiment, the magic folk as well.

"We merpeople need the unity now more than ever. Our blood lines are dwindling and our resources drying up. We rely, you see," he paused and the pull on me tightened, "on the willing minds and healthy bodies of humans. For reproductive purposes, of course."

The way he said it sounded so logical. So necessary. So inviting. I almost volunteered right there on the spot.

Dylan stiffened next to me.

"Every time an experiment occurs, those of us that have the resources try and rescue as many of the beings as possible. We very rarely get any humans out alive, but over the years we have created a small conglomeration. Of course, some of those we save are not willing or able to further our cause, but we cannot have the information about a rebellion leaked. So, only those that have been approved will be admitted to the fortress."

As he broke eye contact to gaze out over the ocean, the pull toward him instantly severed. I glanced at Dylan who had his arms crossed tightly over his chest. A muscle pulsed in his cheek, his expression dark.

"You can rest here tonight, Grey," he said. "I prefer the depths of the water. If you need me, I'll know and will come find you."

"Why are you calling her 'Grey'?" Dylan

growled. "In fact, we both have names if you'd bothered to ask."

I raised my eyebrows at the tone in his voice. Obviously, he was not one for forgiving easily. Dylan ignored my look.

The merman answered in his rich, hypnotic voice. "We in the sea do not have traditional land-dwelling names. We recognize and then describe others by their most defining feature. Her eyes are the color of thick fog that swallows unsuspecting seafarers whole. Of storm clouds that wreck and menace from the sky. Of the many shades of the afterlife."

He spoke like it was a deep compliment, but all I heard was that I reminded him of different forms of death. He said no more, and grasping the golden trident, waded out into the sea until he was swallowed by the waves.

The beach was small. There were no signs of animal life, no shells, no tracks through the sand. It was pristine, but also very exposed. The cliffs loomed up behind, fencing us in.

"Are we supposed to sleep out here in the open?"

Dylan did not seem concerned and flung himself down on the sand. I glanced around again and then settled next to him with a heavy sigh. Soft snoring came instantly from his prone form, but I remained awake, digging my hands into the smooth sandy surface, letting the grains run through my fingers.

The sun disappeared and the moon seemed to suddenly appear in the sky. It had always been there of course, silently watching and waiting for the bright light to fade so it could shine. My eyes tracked its slow progress as it crept along in a star-studded sky, competing to be the brightest. The ocean breeze was warm as it softly swirled around us, and everything should have felt perfect. But there was an uneasiness just below the surface and I could sense it.

Dylan's chest rose and fell in a hypnotic rhythm. His face was slack with the warm caress of sleep reddening the olive skin beneath the darkening stubble. My mind tentatively reached back, remembering when he pressed himself against me in the experiment, wrapped his arms securely around me and followed so close he was millimeters from stepping on my toes. The heat had coursed between us. But it was more than the physical warmth. There was comfort there, a feeling of safety. An attachment that buried deeper into both our souls than we were aware of.

Somewhere near midnight Dylan stirred, and I felt his yellow eyes watching me in the dark. "Can't you sleep?" he asked.

"No."

"What are you thinking about?"

I had failed to find my father or to learn the details of what had happened to him. Failed to complete the experiment and return home to the family I had left so I could ask my mother why she had sent us in the first place. And it had all ended with the spirit being captured and banished back to the Chasm. I had pretty much failed in everything I had set out to do.

I sighed. "Life."

"The life you've lived, or the one to come?"

"I don't know which one is worse."

Dylan pulled himself up from the sand and shuffled next to me. He wrapped a comforting arm around my shoulders and squeezed. I struggled to draw breath against the tightness of his embrace, and he loosened his muscles and dropped his arm so that he gently encircled my waist instead.

"Tell me what your ideal date would be. Like if

we could escape from here and return to our lives, but it was a hundred years ago before the separation." He leaned closer and whispered as his lips brushed against my hair. "Where should I take you?"

Dylan was the only good thing that had happened to me. There was no hope of us living a normal life together, but maybe it was okay to dream, at least for now.

"When I was younger, my father would take me to the beach. It wasn't pristine sand and wilderness like this, it was more pebbles and seaweed and frigid air that whipped against you, but it was my favorite place to be. We would go as a family and there would be no experiments or arguments or talk of home. We would just exist. It was different. We were happy."

He kissed my hair and rested his head against mine.

"There was a cliff-top walk that I did every day. I would go by myself, as close to the precipice as I dared. The howling wind would dart in and out of my ears and I would imagine it was the voices of seafarers, merpeople, and mythical creatures sending messages to me. And I would gaze out over the limitless expanse of blue horizon and feel re-energized. Like all the events of the past had been cleansed."

The words had barely left my mouth before he bounded to his feet and dragged me up. "Come with me."

We walked along the beach to an indentation in the cliffs, where large white boulders had come free and piled high around its base. He laced his fingers with mine and we climbed up the jagged, snaking path until we came to an invisible ledge. My eyes had not seen the imperfection in the face of the cliff, but his had seen every minute detail etched into its surface.

We gazed out over the ocean together. The wind

was mild, its voice barely whispering in the night air, but the nostalgia serenaded my body with romance.

His hand was warm in mine, and he made an effort to grip me lightly, one rough finger gently stroking the smooth skin at the back of my hand. My breathing quickened before my mind had even decided what to do. My body knew what it wanted.

Turning into him, I ran my hands slowly up his chest, feeling his muscles tense at my touch. I pressed myself against him, standing on tiptoes, drawing him closer so his lips met mine. The heat spread through my body, and he responded.

"I don't want to hurt you," he murmured, breath whispering into my mouth.

The desire was strong in his eyes but blended with fear.

"You won't. I trust you," I whispered back.

I pulled his shirt over his head and my hands lingered on the bare skin just above his waistband. Slowly I undid the button of his jeans and slid them down. A throaty growl filled the air, making my heart race in anticipation. His breath was hot and hungry, covering my neck, his stubble tickling my flushed skin as his lips caressed.

He fumbled with the hem of my torn sweater, tightly gripping the fabric. "Are you sure?" he whispered into my hair.

I nodded against him. Gently, he turned me around. His mouth continued to trace patterns on my neck, moving down my shoulder as he unhooked my bra. I murmured softly, drawing in a deep breath as his fingers slid to my breasts, circling the nipples before descending slowly. A tremble ran through him, a vulnerability that made me want him more. Heat followed his fingertips and surged between my legs. He pressed hard against my back, coaxing a moan from between my parted lips.

His rough hands gripped my hips, holding me tight as his mouth slid along my shoulders, teeth grazing my flushed skin. I arched up and into him, barely feeling the sharp points of his teeth as he sank them into my neck. We moved together, the swells growing stronger until a surge gripped my body and rushed over me.

He murmured a growl of pleasure, hot against my ear, the vibrations pouring over my skin. His teeth sunk deeper into my neck, warm blood trickling down my back. He shuddered against me, his fangs cutting through muscle and spearing into my nerves. White hot pain lanced down my spine penetrating my core, so tightly bound with pleasure I whimpered.

Gradually he released his grip on my neck, nuzzling into my skin. We stood together watching the dark ocean, our bodies united as one.

This was peace, this was comfort, this was trust. And if I'd met him before this experiment, before we were forced together, I would have never believed it possible.

He led me carefully back down to the beach. When my feet sank into the soft sand, he paused. His honey eyes gazed deeply into mine, hands running lightly over my shoulders. "Anna," he whispered, "I'm in love with you."

My breathing stopped and stomach flipped with sudden anxiety. There was something about the way he said it. Something wrong. His fingertips brushed the fresh puncture wounds on my neck, a large bruise already congealed under the skin. I flinched involuntarily, unable to hide the grimace.

He held my eyes a moment longer before looking away. "But I can't be with you," he said, voice cracking. "We can never do this again."

Unable to respond, I just blinked at him. The waves crashed and screamed around me, where before they had been so tranquil. His hands dropped from my body, sucking the warmth out of me as they went. The icy fingers of the sea breeze stepped in to embrace me instead.

As he walked away down the beach, even my eyes didn't follow him. My body started to shut down around me, protecting what it had left. But it was too late. I curled up on the chilly sand and watched blindly as the water inched its way toward me and the moon crept slowly out of the sky.

My family had voted against me. My father had left this world and chosen not to communicate with me even though he had been preparing me to do just that. Chris had decided to kill me, to save himself.

And now Dylan was just another person to add to the list of those who didn't want me.

Chapter Thirty-Eight

The morning sun held no warmth as it tried to reach out and comfort me. Standing with arms tightly folded, I stared out to sea, perched in the bow of the small boat. Eventually the tousled blond hair of the merman emerged from the pristine water. He seemed unsurprised to see me waiting for him. His green eyes shone warmly, and my heart lifted slightly at the sight of him.

"Where is Red?"

My mouth tightened in response, and I looked back out to sea. From the corner of my eye, he strummed the tines of the trident like strings on a harp. No noise reached my ears, but a message had been sent. Heavy footfalls crunched on the sand behind me whilst I kept stubbornly focused on the ocean.

Dylan chose to sit on the floor of the boat, close to my feet. His back was against the side, body angled away from me. The merman eased the boat into the water, wading alongside it in the now choppy water and then gracefully sprang to his position in the stern. He deftly steered us away from the beach, past the swirling current, and back into the open ocean.

We glided along perpendicular to the shoreline, the cliffs shrinking behind us, hiding away their faces. The coastline stretched for miles. Sometimes sandy beach greeted the ocean and at other times barren scrubland, the small plants and bushes permanently broken and bent-backed from the corrosive salty air. In the distance, the blue peaks of mountains materialized. Dark, grey mist swirled around them, and from the highest points sparkling white snow glittered in the sunlight.

"Almost there, Grey," the merman said, knowing what had caught my attention.

Dylan glanced over at me, but I stared resolutely away from him. I was sure that if I asked him to, the merman would throw him overboard. The thought gave me a little solace. Dylan turned his face back away from mine and resumed watching the floor. In my peripheral vision, his body slumped.

The small boat steered back toward the shore, the water changing from a deep black to an almost transparent crystal blue. Pebbles and seashells littered the seabed, giving texture to the smooth golden sand. The merman dipped his trident back into the water and the boat knifed through the current and sped toward the mouth of a wide river.

We continued along, drifting upstream and getting progressively higher as the day wore on. The air became thinner and colder, and my eyes kept darting to Dylan's warm arms. This only made me as furious with myself as I was with him, and I crossed my arms over my chest and pressed my legs into the sheltered edge of the boat.

I didn't understand his behavior. He had been pushing me away ever since he arrived on the boat. He said he was glad I had run. That I had saved myself. But maybe he was now feeling the hurt that I had abandoned him after all. Even though he seemed to only have two main emotions—anger and lust—it was so difficult to read him.

We were now high up in the looming mountains. The mist circled around us, its winding, flickering form reminded me of the Chasm, and then of the spirit now trapped down there. It was difficult to see very far ahead but so far nothing that looked remotely like a fortress emerged from the gloom.

"Grey," the merman called softly, "come and sit with me."

Dylan's head whipped around, a fleeting look of

panic on his face. Not making eye contact with him, I moved down the boat and toward the merman. He lifted me up gently, his hands cold and wet as they touched my waist and sat me on the back of the boat.

"I thought you'd want to see this," he said. "There will come a time when you will want to visit with me."

He was looking off into the distance and as we rounded a bend in the river the fog cleared, and a towering waterfall rose above us. The rumble of water suddenly so loud in my ears after the suppressed quiet of the thick mist. The water pounded down onto the small pool below, droplets covering me with a fine layer of freezing spray. The mist danced and spun at the foot of the falls, white and sparkling in the late sunshine.

"There is a portal here that will take you directly to the ocean. If you need to find me, come here and let your soul guide you."

Dylan grumbled quietly, the sound blending with the roaring of the water. The boat moved out from under the waterfall's flowing hair and chose a narrow tributary that wound away toward the west. The fog did not return but the air remained chilly and now my damp clothes leeched even more of my precious body heat away. I slid down and onto the seat by the merman's feet. Bringing my knees up to my chin, I pressed my face down and clenched my jaw hard to stop my teeth from chattering.

I only looked up when the boat lightly touched against the shore and the rocking motion halted. Extending his moist hand, the merman helped me out of the boat. My legs wobbled and the ground seemed to rock and swell as violently as the ocean had. My stomach churned as I knelt on the ground, head pressed against the damp mud until the nausea subsided.

Dylan hovered behind me, but he made no move to comfort me. The merman seemed unfazed. If he dealt with enough humans, sea sickness would probably not be a surprise to him. I pushed into the sticky mud with my hands and staggered to my feet.

"I go no further with you," the merman said. "Follow the path to the fortress. We will meet again in the sea, Grey."

He squeezed my hand, a confident smile on his face. Then he lightly sprang back into the boat, dipped his trident into the water and flowed away.

"Don't fall for it, Anna." Dylan almost spat the words at the retreating boat.

Still feeling the world spinning around me, I snapped back at him. "Thanks for your concern. I do seem to have a habit of falling for the charm of monsters."

His mouth turned down and his eyes opened wide and sorrowfully like a puppy that had been kicked. Ignoring the faint clawing of my conscience, I forced my focus toward the trail and made my legs walk.

"Maybe you should rest a while," he whispered. "You look pretty green."

Ignoring him I stomped over the mud and shrubs toward the gravel trail which snaked up and around the mountainside. Each switchback alternated between the weak warmth of the setting sun and the frigid air of the shadows.

The trail ascended sharply, the way littered with loose scree which screamed and echoed as it tumbled back down, collecting more debris like an avalanche. Placing every foot carefully, I tested the weight of my foot on solid earth before releasing the other, making sure I didn't trip so he wouldn't need to catch me. I didn't know if he knew what I was doing or if he was thinking about something else, but a ghost of a smile flitted across his face as he watched.

My body betrayed me again. As I caught the softening of his expression, the tenderness in his eyes, the corners of my mouth turned up and my breath hitched. My irritation rose immediately afterward at the weakening. I stopped walking and stood with my hands on hips, body blocking his path up the trail.

"Why, Dylan?"

His eyes held mine, but he didn't say anything.

"Were you just playing the game after all?"

His mouth tightened and his almond pupils narrowed to feline slits. He still didn't offer an explanation or give an excuse. His gaze dropped to the floor and his posture slumped. But what really made my heart retreat back into the safe confines of my chest, was that he didn't deny it. I nodded, although he wasn't looking at me anymore and continued up the mountainside.

As the sun finally disappeared, plunging us into a chilly twilight, the path ended. We were on a ledge carved out of stone. The trail fell away behind us, and the gaping openness of the mountainside plummeted down in front. The only solidity was a large stone door, set into the sheer face of the mountain.

The wind gusted strongly, ripped at my hair, and shook my body. The dusky light faintly illuminated a carving etched onto the door. It was the silhouette of a flower. The soft, understated shape of a poppy. Each of the six petals bore a different ensign with the intricate swirls of the Celtic knot in the center.

On one of the petals the familiar outline of two human hands pressed together, the thumbs forming a heart shape. The second held the flickering outline of a flame, and another the three-pronged trident. The demi-beings were represented by the outline of half a human hand, the other half the unmistakable shape of a cloven hoof. A quadrant square with a sun, moon, tree, and skull was etched onto the bottom petal. The final held a teardrop shape. Most would look at it and think water but knowing who it represented, it had to be blood.

The door creaked open, the stone protesting noisily in the silent evening. Rays of warm, flickering light snuck out and crept toward us. Illuminated in the doorway stood the red eyes of the seal that had cavorted next to me in the ocean. Now in human form, the selkie welcomed us in with a small wave of his dark hand, like the swivel of a flipper. He still wore no clothes, similar to Amura's memory that I had watched so avidly back in the experiment, and I kept my eyes politely raised to his face, knowing that my cheeks were pink despite my best efforts.

As we moved inside toward the warmth and light, Dylan put his hand gently on my waist, pushing me sideways and took the position in between the selkie and me. I rolled my eyes, unsurprised, and moved away from his touch. He raised his eyebrows pointedly back at me. Noticing, as Dylan wasn't exactly subtle, the selkie barked out a laugh. Being so close to him the odor of fish swirled into my nostrils and the sharp, tapered points on each of his teeth winked at me.

"She's perfectly safe here, werewolf. Miss Anna has been designated 'off limits'. She's protected." His red eyes travelled down Dylan's body, taking in his tense shoulders and clenched fists. "Possibly a fact that you should start to consider also, I think."

The only effect this seemed to have was to make him worse, and constant grumbling emanated from him as we continued. The door closed behind us with another loud series of grating and complaining noises as it scraped along the stone.

The walls and floor were hewn out of the

mountainside, leaving the rocky edges uneven and textured. The place was well lit with deeply set sconces and dancing firelights as we traveled further inwards. It was eerily like the Chasm. The smell being also musty and damp as we progressed.

The only redeeming feature was the open ceiling. Instead of a grey rock roof, the top of the mountain had been cut away. The stars twinkled in the black sky and the airiness made the space feel open and calming. There was an enchantment of some kind preventing the howling wind from entering and this kept the warmth inside as well.

Quiet footsteps padded up to us from a small tributary that joined the main passageway. As soon as I saw the flame-red hair, my heart leapt, and I threw myself on her, wrapping my arms tightly around her cold, smooth neck.

"I'm so glad you made it!" I enthused in her ear.

Having taken her by surprise she seemed to come to her senses. She placed a strong hand on each of my arms and prized me off. She pinned my arms to my sides, leaning back as far as she could to create as much space as possible between us.

"Yes, I see that." Her face held the cool, calm exterior she always did, but her eyes gave her away as they flashed in amusement. "There is someone who needs to see you. Dylan, go and find your chamber. Human, with me."

She turned without waiting, her icy handprints lingering on my skin. Not bothering to see the protest that was surely etched onto Dylan's face, I followed. The selkie melted away down another tunnel, thankfully taking with him the strong smell of fish.

I pummeled her with questions. What happened? How did she get here? How long had this been planned?

She answered none of them. Eventually as her lack of response seemed not to deter me from continuing to ask, she halted and spun to face me.

Usually, the aggressive posture, intrusion of personal space and introduction of her pointed canines into a conversation tended to silence the other party. But I knew her well enough by now. I gave her my most innocent smile, raised my eyebrows slightly in anticipation of an answer and leaned in closer.

If she'd known how to roll her eyes, I think she would have.

Instead, she said, "No more questions, human."

We had arrived outside another carved door. This one had a mountain scene etched onto it. Tall snow-capped peaks set in front of a dipping sun, the shadows of soaring birds within the clear sky. In the foreground, lush grass covered the floor, strewn with wildflowers. A small river completed the picture, winding its way around the side of the mountain and flowing into a wide stream at the bottom.

Amura nudged me and I knocked at the door. The hard stone sent jolts of pain through my cold hands. An echoing sound of hooves approached from within, and the door eased open.

Framed in the doorway was a being I had never seen before. His skin was a light mauve, torso bare in the glow from the torches. His body bore the powerful, carved muscles of a mountain goat, tan fur rippling down. Four dainty cloven hooves stood perfectly square on the threshold. His eyes were brown, set slightly too laterally on his face, pupils horizontal black slits. A brown goatee tufted from his chin and a wide smile graced his face.

I should have liked him straight away. His attitude was welcoming, his aura understatedly charismatic. But my eyes travelled down his muscular arm, to the hand that was grasped in his mauve one. The gesture natural to them, spoke volumes to the observer. Of a tender and loving relationship where both parties treated the other as an equal.

My head slowly lifted. My breath stopped as an invisible force wound around me, squeezing like a vice. I looked into the familiar grey eyes.

"Welcome to the revolution, Anna," my father said.

The End

www.nkbrownauthor.com

NK BROWN

I am a veterinarian and a proud mother of three. Originally from Stratford-Upon-Avon I now live outside of Boston.

Finally ready for the career change I have always wanted, I joined Jericho Writers and am an alumni of their Ultimate Novel Writing Course 2023/24. I love to write in the SFF genre usually with a dark and speculative twist. An animal or two will usually pop up somewhere in my writing!

When not reading or writing or reading about writing, you can find me out on a long run, lost in my imagination (or a good audiobook) as I plan my next novel.

Follow me on socials: X/Bluesky @Nattykbrown and Instagram @nkbrownauthor

NK BROWN

Evernight Teen ®

www.evernightteen.com